# CURRIED LOBSTER MURDER

## THE DARLING DELI SERIES, BOOK 14

PATTI BENNING

SUMMER PRESCOTT BOOKS PUBLISHING

# CHAPTER ONE

For what must have been the hundredth time since she'd received it six weeks ago, Moira Darling pulled up the email congratulating her on being chosen as one of the lucky seven contestants in the Grand Cruise Chef War. In just two more days, she would be boarding a plane for Florida, where the cruise ship would leave port, and she was feeling completely overwhelmed.

"The first order from Zander Marsh is coming today, isn't it?" Meg Brownell, one of Moira's employees, asked from the kitchen doorway.

"Yes, it is. It should be here by four," she told the

young woman, putting away her phone and turning her attention back to the present for the time being.

"Good, because we're almost out of milk, and Dante's worried because he needs it to make the quiches tomorrow morning."

"You can promise him that in just a few short hours, he'll have all of the fresh, organic milk that he could dream of."

The deli owner smiled, easily able to imagine the young man's concern over his precious quiches. Though he had only been working for her at Darling's DELIcious Delights for a little over six months, Dante was one of her most valuable employees. He was a natural chef, and needed very little direction in the kitchen. Though he wasn't quite as confident with the customers as her manager Darrin, he was worth his weight in gold as a valued member of her team.

Meg was his girlfriend, and had begun working at the deli even more recently than Dante. She seemed his opposite in many ways; she was naturally outgoing and talkative, and preferred to follow recipes than to improvise her own creations, but despite their differences, the two of them made a strong couple. Moira was glad that their relationship seemed to be going strong, and was happy to let them share shifts as long as they continued to focus on work while they were at the deli.

Allison, her newest employee, was currently in the next town over helping Moira's daughter, Candice, figure out a new business plan for her store, Candice's Candies, before the cruise. Just a few weeks ago, the young woman had begun offering homemade, custom-shaped chocolates and candies for sale online, and her sales had been through the roof ever since. Moira wasn't surprised—her daughter was as skilled at making sweets as she herself was at making soup, and her prices were unbeatable.

All in all, things were going smoothly and it was a

great time for Moira to be gone for a while. However, even though she knew that her employees could handle pretty much anything that happened at the deli, she was still anxious at the thought of being out of reach for so long. To make matters worse, she was also going to be leaving her two dogs, Maverick and Keeva, at home.

Normally Candice would watch the dogs for her, but the free cruise included a spot for each contestant to bring a guest, so Moira had jumped at the chance to spend ten days in the Caribbean with her daughter. Luckily, David Morris, the private detective that she had been dating since the winter before, had agreed to stay at her place and watch the dogs, but she knew she'd still miss the furry company of Maverick and Keeva.

*I can't believe my name actually got drawn,* she thought. *When I entered the drawing, I didn't think there was a chance that I would get chosen. What did I get myself into?* The cruise wasn't just a cruise—it was also a competition between chefs, and the prizes were high stakes. The winner would receive ten thousand dollars, and be featured on a segment of a celebrity cooking show. Moira doubted the challenges would be easy, and she was certain that the other chefs would be far more skilled than she was. In an effort not to stress herself out, she was determined to focus on enjoying the cruise over winning the competition, though of course she would still try her hardest when the time came. She was a Darling, after all.

When the delivery finally arrived a few hours later, Moira hurried out back with her employees to greet the truck driver. It was Zander Marsh himself; a tall, bald man in his thirties whose passions included brewing beer and seeking more efficient and modern methods of farming. At first, his personality had rubbed the deli owner the wrong way, but after a few meetings—and the realization that he wasn't a murderer—she had realized that he was actually a good guy at heart. It was rare to find someone as passionate about their line of work as he was, and even more rare to find someone willing to work with small businesses like hers on an individual basis.

*This is why it's important to have a good relationship with the people you do business with,* she thought as she watched him carefully back up the rest of the way to the deli's side door. *When you treat people well, they tend to treat you well in return.*

"It's so nice of you to drive this over yourself," she said once the truck had been shut off and Zander had hopped down to greet them.

"I thought it would be the only way to make sure that everything was perfect for the first delivery," he said. "You're officially my first customer, now that old Mr. Samwell's farm is mine."

"Well, it's an honor," she said. "And I'm sure every-thing will be perfect."

"Did you reconsider what I asked you at our last meeting?" he asked as he unlatched the truck's loading door and heaved it open.

Moira frowned and thought about her reply as she watched her employees begin unloading the truck. Zander wanted to know if she was interested in selling some of the beer and ale that he brewed himself, at the deli. She wasn't sure yet if she wanted to deal with the hassle of getting a license to sell liquor, or even if the sales would be worth the extra time and money it would take to get the project rolling.

"I need some more time to think about it," she told him as she stepped forward to take a box from Dante, who was making sure the refrigerated goods got out of the truck first.

"Okay, just know that the offer still stands," he replied. "I really want to start getting my name out there, even if I'm just selling locally at first."

She nodded, deciding to do some research on what

it would take. She enjoyed supporting local brands, and had always been grateful when other local businesses supported her. *As soon as I get home,* she thought, *I'll get on the computer and look up what it would take to get a liquor license for this place—if I even can.* Suddenly she remembered a very important delivery that she had promised to make tonight, and realized that Zander would just have to wait a little while longer to get an answer. Tonight was the night that the last puppy was going home.

Two months ago, a very pregnant Labrador retriever had been abandoned behind Darling's DELIcious Delights. Moira had taken her in, and before she knew it, she had six chubby little puppies in her mudroom. She had spent the last few weeks trying desperately to find forever homes for all six of them. Zander had taken one, and between her and all of her friends asking the people they knew, homes had been found for the other five. Thankfully David's sister had fallen in love with their mother, Hazel, and the older dog had gone home with Karissa a few days ago. This evening would mark the bittersweet departure of the last puppy, and the first time in weeks that Moira would be able to get a good night's rest.

"How is Flower doing?" she asked Zander once the last of the food had been brought inside. He had taken the littlest puppy, the only yellow one in the litter. He had named her Sunflower, which had quickly gotten shortened to Flower.

"She's great," he said with a genuine smile. "Even though it's only been a few days, she seems perfectly happy at the farm with me. She's the sweetest little thing."

"I'm happy that you decided to take her," Moira admitted. "She's my favorite puppy, and I'm looking forward to hearing your updates about her."

It had been hard to resist the urge to keep any of the puppies for herself, but she knew that between her work schedule and her other two dogs, it would be hard to give the puppy the time, attention, and training it deserved. *Not to mention the cruise I'm about to go on,* she thought. *It wouldn't be fair to ask David to watch a little puppy in addition to Maverick and Keeva.*

"I'll email you pictures every week," he promised. "I bet she'll be growing like a weed soon. It won't be long before she's a real farm dog."

Once Zander left, Moira and her employees spent the next few hours putting away the newly delivered food, serving customers, and going over last-minute instructions for the deli while she was away. There seemed to be an endless number of instructions; most of the time everything went smoothly, but occasional disasters, both major and minor, did happen. The deli owner knew that with her luck, the second she boarded that plane, the deli would begin to suffer under Murphy's law. So, knowing that it was probably overkill, but deciding that it was better to be over-prepared than under- she went over all of the emergency procedures again. She reminded them what the security cameras covered, and how to access the footage if they needed it, and also left them numbers for both David and Detective Jefferson. Given the deli's track record, she wasn't prepared to risk anything.

When it was time to close down and leave for the day, Moira took a deep breath and looked around. This was the last time she would be in the deli for over a week. Tomorrow would be spent packing, doing some last-minute shopping—if she was going to be in the Caribbean, she needed at least one good bathing suit—and getting David settled in at her house since he would be staying there with the dogs until she got back. The next morning, they would be leaving bright and early so he could drop her and Candice off at the airport... and then they would be on their way at last.

# CHAPTER TWO

Moira's alarm went off hours before sunrise. She had only gotten a few hours' worth of sleep, and she knew she would probably pay for it later, but she could always sleep on the three-hour flight to Miami.

Quickly pulling on the clothes that she had laid out the night before—shorts and a tee shirt in expectation of the warmer weather in Florida—she shushed the excited dogs.

"David's still sleeping downstairs," she told them in a whisper. "We have to be quiet. He doesn't need to wake up until right before we leave, and I'm sure he'll appreciate the extra sleep."

Even though the dogs couldn't comprehend what she had said, they seemed to respond to her low tones, and their whining quieted. The deli owner slowly opened the bedroom door and made the dogs follow her out into the hallway instead of dashing forward and racing down the stairs like they usually did.

Once downstairs in the kitchen with the dogs safely outside—it felt weird not to have to maneuver around the baby gate that had kept the puppies contained in the mudroom—she turned the coffee maker on and pulled out the list that she had made for herself yesterday.

"Well, all of my clothes are packed," she muttered to herself, reading the list. "And I'll finish packing the other stuff soon."

Her big suitcase was already waiting for her by the front door, but she had yet to pack her carry on or figure out what she would need in her purse. All of that would have to wait until after she had finished her first cup of coffee. She let the dogs back in, and went upstairs.

Next on the list was a reminder to leave the emergency credit card on the counter for David, which she did. The account was strictly for emergency vet trips. After two separate middle-of-the-night trips that had unexpectedly cost her a few thousand dollars, she had decided that a backup plan wasn't only smart; it was necessary. On the off chance that one of the dogs got hurt or sick while she was gone, she wanted David to have access to the card. Since nearly everything on the cruise was already paid for by the company hosting the competition, she doubted she would even need to access her bank account.

The last item on the list was a reminder to eat something. She made a face, but couldn't very well be annoyed at herself for thinking ahead. It was true that she wasn't hungry right now, but by the time the plane was in the air, and certainly by the time they had landed, she would be starved. Wishing that they had time to stop at the deli for one of Dante's famous quiches, she got up and made herself a bowl of oatmeal instead.

By the time she had finished her last-minute packing, fed the dogs, and wolfed down her quick breakfast, David was up as well. He looked tired, but gave her a smile as he sat down at the kitchen table across from her.

"Excited?" he asked.

"Definitely. I don't get away enough; this week should be fun."

"Are you nervous about the competition at all?"

"If I let myself think about it, I am," she admitted. "I don't really know what to expect, and I'm sure a lot of the other people there will be more experienced than I am. I just like making soup, putting together sandwiches, and whipping up the occasional pot roast. The other contestants are probably all people with actual sit-down restaurants, with full menus and more variety than my little deli could ever offer."

"I think you'll do just fine against them," he said confidently. "You seriously have a gift when it comes to food. You can take just about any bunch of ingredients and mix them together to make something delicious."

"I think you're a little bit biased," she said, but she was smiling. It was always nice to hear a compliment, especially from someone who she cared so much about, like David.

"That I am." He grinned, then covered her hand

with his. "But I'm being honest when I say you don't have anything to worry about."

"Thank you," she said, blushing now. "That means a lot."

She cleared her throat and looked down at the dogs, about to ask him if he needed her to go over anything else when she saw first Maverick's and then Keeva's ears perk up. A moment later, both the German shepherd and Irish wolfhound were stampeding down the hall toward the front door.

"I'm guessing Candice is here," she said with a laugh, rising. She was always amazed by how sensitive the dogs' senses were, and how they seemed to be able to tell the different cars apart just by sound. In her opinion they were a better alarm system than anything technology could offer, and they were great companions to boot.

She opened the door and greeted her daughter and Eli. Candice gave a big yawn before stepping inside.

"This is way too early to be up," she said.

"You know I'm not a morning person either, but it's worth it for the cruise," her mother pointed out. "Just think, by this evening we'll be sitting on a cruise ship gradually making our way into the tropics. Then you can sleep in as late as you want."

"As if," the young woman said with a laugh. "I'm not going to miss any of this trip due to sleep if I can help it. I'll just have to catch up when we get back."

Moira smiled, glad that her daughter was so excited for the trip. It would be wonderful to spend some time relaxing together. Since Candice had quit working at the deli in favor of opening her own shop, the two of them hadn't been able to spend as much time together. She was sure her daughter enjoyed the independence that came with supporting herself, but that didn't stop the deli owner from missing her.

"Do either of you want a bowl of oatmeal?" she asked, looking between Candice and Eli as they came in and shut the door behind themselves. "It won't take long to make."

Both of them did, so Moira hurried into the kitchen to make the food, conscious that they had to leave soon if they were going to make it to the airport as early as she wanted to. *Well, we're planning on getting there two hours early, so we should have a little bit of leeway,* she thought. *Still, I won't be able to relax until we're sitting at the gate.*

Twenty minutes later, the oatmeal was eaten, the bowls were cleaned, the deli owner had finished packing her last-minute necessities, and Candice and Eli were murmuring to each other in the hallway as Moira and David brought the suitcases out to her green SUV.

"I love you," Candice said to Eli as she got into the back seat of the SUV. "I'm going to miss you so much. Take good care of Felix, okay?"

"I love you too, and I'll make sure to give him extra treats, though I know it won't make up for him missing you. Will you text me when you land?"

The deli owner smiled at the obvious love between the two young people. They hadn't known each other for more than a few months, but that didn't seem to matter. She was glad that her daughter had finally found someone that seemed to be a genuinely good person. She could only hope that their relationship would keep going strong.

"Ready?" David asked her, slipping his arm around

her waist and brushing a kiss across her cheek. "We'll be right on schedule if we leave now."

She nodded.

"Let's get going," she said.

A couple of hours later, Moira said her own hurried goodbyes to David at the security checkpoint, wishing that she had time for more than a quick kiss and 'I love you,' but construction on the way to the airport had already slowed them down, and the security lines looked long.

"I'll give you a call when we land," she promised. "But I won't be able to use my phone once the cruise ship leaves shore. I have my tablet though, and I'll email you and have Candice show me how to do a video call."

"I look forward to it," he said. "I want you to have a good time and be safe. And Moira? Try to stay out of trouble."

# CHAPTER THREE

The flight went as smoothly as Moira could have hoped. They went through security without a single issue, making her glad that she had gone over the airline's requirements multiple times as she was packing. She and Candice had seats together on the plane. Letting her daughter take the window seat, the deli owner settled herself in the middle one after stashing her carry on in the compartment above her head. She turned her phone off, pulled out the novel she had picked up at a recent library book sale, and settled down to wait as the rest of the passengers loaded up, glancing over at Candice occasionally to make sure she was okay. The young woman looked calm enough. She had her headphones plugged into the seat-back screen and was flipping through the free movie choices.

"Excited?" Moira asked when her daughter looked over.

"Yeah." She grinned. "Thanks so much for inviting me. This is going to be awesome."

"I hope so." She smiled back, but couldn't ignore the niggling worry that had been chewing at her since she learned that her name had been drawn. Was she ready for this? Would she be able to be a real competitor in the competition, or would the other chefs all be far more skilled than she was? Was she just going to embarrass herself?

Her doubts didn't matter—the captain was speaking, the plane's engines were revving, and before she knew it, they were in the air.

After landing in Florida, things seemed to blur

together. The two women retrieved their bags from the luggage carousel, then somehow managed to find the bus company that would drive them straight to the docks.

The cruise ship, when it finally came into view, was huge. Its name, *Caribbean Queen*, was written on the side in huge letters. As she realized this enormous boat would be her home for the next week, Moira replaced her worries about the coming competition with far less rational fears. How could this thing even float? What if they struck some submerged rock and went down like the *Titanic*? *Don't be silly,* she thought, taking deep breaths. *The people who built this thing knew what they were doing. Of course it floats; it's floating now, isn't it? And we have all sorts of underwater sonar and cameras these days that they didn't have back when the* Titanic *sank. We'll be perfectly fine. Just relax and have fun.*

Deciding to obey her own command, she hefted her bags and gave Candice a broad smile. It was time to embark on their adventure at last.

Boarding the ship was surprisingly similar to boarding an airplane. They went through metal detectors in a long, slow-moving line, then gave their luggage to porters, who put the bags in big wheeled bins with a promise that the suitcases would be delivered to their rooms that evening.

The crowds made things confusing at first, but Moira and Candice did their best to follow the signs for the Grand Cruise Chef War, and soon enough found themselves in a large room with a banner welcoming the contestants on board. A sharply dressed woman with short, spiky brown hair and a tablet in her hand approached them.

"Names?" she asked them.

"Moira Darling and Candice Darling-Thomson," the deli owner said. She watched as the other woman's fingers flew across the tablet's touch screen. A moment later, she smiled.

"Welcome aboard, Ms. Darling and Ms. Darling-Thomson. Mother and daughter, I presume?" They nodded. "My name is Charlene Edwards. You can call me Charlie or Miss Edwards, whichever you prefer. It's my job to get you settled in and answer any questions that you have."

"It's nice to meet you," Moira said. "Neither of us have ever been on a cruise before, so I'm sure you'll have your work cut out for you. I guess my first question is, where are our rooms?"

"Right this way," the other woman said. "All of the contestants have rooms on this floor—the third floor —to make matters easier for them. Both the kitchen and the banquet hall that we'll be using for the competition are also on this floor."

She led them down a hallway as she spoke, and Moira tried to pay attention to the layout of the ship as she listened to the other woman's explanation. She was sure she would get lost a few times before figuring out how to get around, but thankfully there were maps at each corner, and they passed a couple of stewards on the way to their rooms.

The rooms were adjoining, each the mirror of the other. They were simple, but looked comfortable. There was a full-sized bed in each, along with one window that looked out over the ocean, plenty of shelf and wardrobe space, a desk, and a small private bathroom. Everything looked clean and fresh, and the deli owner and her daughter exchanged smiles.

"Your luggage will be brought up later," Charlie was saying. "It will be in your rooms by the time that you're back from dinner. Speaking of meals, tonight we will be dining in the banquet hall that is put aside for the Chef War, but most of your meals will be eaten in one of the dining halls with the rest of the guests. We also have a couple of twenty-four hour buffets, and the ship does offer room service at all times. There's a small packet on your nightstands that will explain the dining options in more detail."

"What time is dinner tonight?" Moira asked.

"The banquet hall opens at five-thirty, and we begin the first course at six. Which means you have..." She glanced at her sleek wristwatch, "an hour and a half. At the banquet we will go over the rules of the competition, you'll receive the information you'll need for the first challenge—which takes place tomorrow morning—and you'll also meet the rest of the contestants as well as the judges."

"Are you one of the judges?"

"No, no, I'm just an assistant," she said with a smile. "My job is to make sure everyone knows what's going on and gets to where they need to be at the right times. I'm available to answer your questions at any time of day or night, so don't hesitate to hunt me down if you need something. I'm in room three-oh-eight, which is right by the banquet hall, if you need me."

They listened as Charlie gave them directions to the banquet hall— "It's on the port side of the ship, with a huge sign out front. You can't miss it."— then handed Moira her photo tag that would identify her as a contestant in the Chef War. When the other woman left them, they tested their room keys, hefted their purses, and went into their separate rooms to begin getting ready for the dinner later that evening.

The day of traveling had worn the deli owner out, but there wasn't quite enough time for a nap before dinner. Instead of lying down and risking falling asleep, the deli owner decided to send an email to David and check on how the deli was doing. It was only her first day away from home, but she felt as if she had been gone for much longer. It was amazing to think that just this morning she had woken up in her bed in Maple Creek back in Michigan, and now she was on a cruise ship in Florida about to depart for a tour of the Caribbean islands.

Once she got her tablet hooked up to the ship's Wi-Fi, she attached the keyboard and sat down at the small desk. She decided to check for any emails from Darrin first—she wouldn't be able to stop worrying until she knew everything was going smoothly at the deli. She hadn't received any calls from Darling's DELIcious Delights since she got off the plane, but it wasn't until she logged into her work email that she breathed a sigh of relief. No news could only be good news.

Next she logged into her personal email and started a message to David, telling him about her day in more detail than she had been able to during their hurried phone call earlier; she did her best describing how amazing—and intimidating—the enormous ship was. She ended the email by asking how the dogs were doing and, smiling, added an *I love you* to the end. She pressed send, then got up to take a quick shower. In no time at all she would be meeting her chef opponents as well as the judges, and she was determined to make a good impression.

# CHAPTER FOUR

By the time she emerged from the shower, someone had delivered her suitcase. *Good, I can change into something nice*, she thought, tucking the towel around herself. She had packed a couple of different dresses, and decided to go with a simple olive green one for tonight. She was saving her best dress, a sleek black one, for the final ceremony, when they would hand over the $10,000 check to the winner. She knew that the chances of actually winning weren't very high, but it would be good to look nice regardless.

As she pulled on her dress and slipped her feet into strappy brown sandals, she had a sudden moment of panic. What would the other contestants be wearing? What would they be like? She knew that any form of competition could bring out the worst in some people, and with the stakes this high, at least some of the contestants were bound to be less than friendly. She had hoped to make some friends while on the cruise, but was now realizing that might not be so likely.

*We're all adults,* she thought as she finished buckling her sandals. *I'm sure this competition won't turn us into monsters.*

Just as Charlie had promised, the banquet hall was easy to find. In front of the heavy oak doors was a large banner welcoming them to the Second Annual Chef War hosted by Grand Cruise Lines. A steward opened the doors for her and Candice after checking Moira's tag and gestured them in.

The hall was beautiful. It had high ceilings with several gorgeous chandeliers, large windows that currently looked out over the harbor, and even a balcony for outdoor dining. On one side of the room was a stage, holding a long table—she assumed the judges would sit there. The rest of the floor was covered by smaller round tables for the contestants and their guests. Servers were making the rounds, delivering drinks and appetizers to those already seated.

"Ms. Darling?" one of the servers said, peering at her ID tag hanging from a lanyard around her neck. "Right this way. You're seated over by the window. Each table seats six, so you'll have two other people joining you."

She led them over to a round table where a middle-aged woman and an elderly man were already seated. Moira sat down in the spot indicated by a name card. She felt a thrill at the sight of her name printed in curling script on the thick paper. It felt so official, and so final. There was no backing out now.

"Hi, I'm Nadine Jenkins," the woman said, giving her a nervous smile. "I'm one of the contestants."

The woman had mousy brown hair that curled around her shoulders. Her floral print dress was clean, but looked worn, and Moira noticed that she kept chewing on her lower lip; a nervous tic that left it red and irritated.

"Moira Darling," the deli owner said, extending her hand, which the woman grasped and then released in a quick shake. "I'm a contestant too. This is my daughter, Candice."

"This is my father, Doug," Nadine said. "My husband had to stay home and watch the kids, so he offered to come with me."

"Nice to meet you, Doug." Moira smiled at him, then turned her attention back to Nadine. "So, what do you do? I know each of the contestants has to either own or work at some sort of restaurant. I own a deli up in Michigan."

"I own a small diner in Minnesota," the other woman said. "Well, my husband is the one that owns it. I just run it."

"That sounds nice. It must be wonderful to work together as a family like that. Do your kids help out too?"

"They're too young," Nadine told her. "The oldest is twelve. She helps out with the dishes sometimes."

"Well, just a few more years and I bet she'll be doing a lot more," the deli owner assured her. "Candice here was a great help at the deli while she worked there. She owns her own business now though."

"Oh, that's nice." The woman gave them a small smile. If she was going to say anything else, it got interrupted by the arrival of another set of people.

The older of the two, a man in his fifties, introduced himself as Bobby Babcock. The woman, who looked to be Moira's age, was his wife, Linda. They owned a burger joint on the East Coast, and both of them looked very happy to be there.

"Our son is in charge of the restaurant while we're gone," Linda told them. "I'm so proud of him. For a long time, we were worried that he wouldn't want to take over the restaurant when we retired, but he's finally starting to show some interest."

"That's wonderful," Moira told them.

*Who will take over the deli when it's time for me to retire?* she wondered as the others picked up the conversation. *Darrin, maybe? Does he really want to spend the rest of his life working at the deli?* She wondered how different her life would have been if she hadn't gotten divorced. It would be so nice to have a real partner in life and work, like these women seemed to have with their husbands.

"You all seem really friendly," said Bobby when the conversation hit a lull. "I have to admit; I wasn't expecting to meet such nice people. With the prize at stake, I was expecting the atmosphere would be more like every person for him- or herself. This is much nicer."

"We're all civilized," the deli owner said with a smile, though she had been worried about the exact same thing not long ago. "I'm sure things will change once the competition starts and people begin getting eliminated."

"Ten thousand dollars is a lot of money," Nadine said, nodding in agreement. "I'd be surprised if people kept on being so civil to each other for the whole week."

"It's not really the money I'm after," Bobby admitted. "It's the cooking segment with a celebrity chef. Something like that could really shoot a restaurant into the big time. We're already doing well enough, of course—we were voted the best burger joint in town a few years back and have won a few local competitions, but nothing like this."

"That's what I'm after too," Moira said. "Not that the money wouldn't be nice but I think the chance to be on TV with a famous chef would be amazing. I haven't really entered any competitions before though, other than one at the local county fair and... well, that didn't turn out so good." She fell silent, hoping that she wouldn't have to remember the horrible few weeks surrounding the soup competition at the county fair. Thankfully Candice asked them what food other than burgers they served at their restaurant, and the conversation turned to talk of which side dish went best with a good burger.

A few minutes later, after the room had filled up with chatter and laughter, Charlie stepped up to the microphone that was standing on the center of the stage in front of the long table.

"Can I have your attention, please?" she asked. A silence fell over the room as all eyes turned toward her. "I would like to welcome each and every one of you to the second annual Grand Cruise Chef War!"

She paused as the room erupted in applause, then continued, "We are very excited to have you here today, and we hope that this next week exceeds your expectations. As most of you already know, my name is Charlie Edwards, and it is my job to make sure that each and every one of you has everything you need to make this trip a trip to remember. In just a moment I will introduce the judges and we will go over some basic rules of the competition. We will then hand out envelopes containing the information you will need for the first challenge which starts tomorrow morning at eight. After that, dinner will be served and you will be free to socialize. But first, I'm going to ask everybody to turn their attention toward the balcony windows. In just a minute, we will be pulling away from the dock and our adventure will officially begin."

Moira, along with every other person in the room, turned her attention to the huge windows out of which they could see the port. She could hear loud music coming from above, where the rest of the guests were probably gathered on deck to witness the moment the huge boat began to move. Strains of a familiar song floated down through the propped open balcony doors, and she grinned, beginning to get into the festive spirit of things. When a large cheer went up and she saw the port outside begin to move, she realized that they must have set sail. She hadn't felt even the smallest jolt as the engines kicked into gear. *This is amazing*, she thought. *I can hardly even tell I'm on a ship.*

She looked over at Candice, who had an ear-to-ear grin on her face, then at her other table mates. Linda looked excited, and was gripping Bobby's arm; he looked eager, if a bit anxious, though nothing like Nadine who was already looking slightly green. Doug, her father, just looked impatient as he picked at his napkin and looked around for a server.

"Very exciting," Charlie said from the stage, clapping as people cheered from their seats. "Another successful cruise has begun. I know you are all probably eager to begin exploring this wonderful ship, but I'm going to have to ask for your patience for a little while longer. First I would like to introduce the man who made all of this possible... Damien Warner."

She stepped aside as a sharply dressed man walked up to the microphone. Moira could tell just by looking at him that he was well off. Everything about him oozed money. He was handsome enough, though his nose looked as if it had been broken at least once in his life. His clothes, however, made up for it. His suit was perfectly tailored and fit him like a glove, and a gold watch sparkled on his wrist. He looked to be about a decade younger than she was, but wore his age much better. As he took the microphone off the stand, he flashed them a charming smile, revealing brilliantly white teeth.

"Welcome aboard," he said, gazing down at them from the stage. "As some of you may suspect from my name, my father is Leslie Warner himself. He owns this ship and one other, the *Caribbean Star*, and even though he is not with us today, I would like to take a moment to thank him, because without his hard work and ambition, none of us would be here today." He raised a glass of water in a toast, and Moira and the other guests followed suit with the drinks they had ordered.

"A couple of years ago," he continued, "I had the idea to host some sort of competition on the cruises. My goal was to help small business owners who have put in the hard work to get where they are today and have the ambition to reach great heights—though of course we also hope to provide entertainment for our other guests. Thanks to some help from my father, we managed to get everything arranged to host the very first Grand Cruise Chef War last year... and it was a hit! I can only hope that this year's competition goes just as well.

"Now to introduce the judges. I will, of course, be serving as the head judge. Ms. Felicity Dane and Mr. Walter Rae are the other two judges this year. Please give them a round of applause."

A thin woman with long blond hair and a tan that didn't quite look real stood up and beamed at them, followed by a stocky, dark-skinned man who offered them a theatrical bow.

"I'm going to let Charlie take over now to explain the rules," Damien said once the smattering of applause had ended and the other two judges had taken their seats. "I swear she knows them better than I do... and I wrote them!"

He handed the microphone back to the woman with spiky brown hair and returned to his seat at the table. Charlie cleared her throat and began speaking, going over the rules of the competition, which were pretty basic. *No cheating,* Moira thought. *That's basically what it boils down to. These rules should be*

*easy enough to follow at least, since I don't have any*
*plans to cheat my way to the prize.*

When she finished, the envelopes with the instructions for the first challenge were handed out. Moira opened hers and was disappointed to see nothing more than a room number and a time she was supposed to arrive. She was hoping to have some time to plan what she was going to make first, but it didn't look like that was going to happen.

At long last the waiters began rolling in carts of food. Her stomach growled as the first course—a small bowl of lobster bisque and a salad with blue cheese, raspberry vinaigrette, and candied pecans—was laid out in front of her. If all of the food on the cruise was this good, she would need to buy some bigger pants by the time they got home.

# CHAPTER FIVE

After finishing her last bite of dessert, a sumptuous lava cake topped with salted caramel sauce, Moira picked up her glass and excused herself from the table. Nadine, Bobby, and Linda had already left, but Candice was deep in discussion with another one of the contestants, a young Mexican woman named Sofia Flores. They were about the same age, and as young entrepreneurs had a lot in common. The deli owner had lost track of the conversation once they started talking about music, and decided to step out onto the balcony to clear her thoughts.

Night had fallen, but the air was still warm and humid with the occasional cooling breeze. She could see the stars, more than she could ever see on land,

and knew the view would be even better from up on deck. She decided to put off stargazing for now, since it was so late and she worried about the first challenge.

She turned back to see Candice and Sofia's conversation wrapping up. Once the two women had said their goodbyes, Candice rose from her seat and looked around the room. There were only two other people still there, besides Sofia; a couple in the opposite corner that was giggling together. They had been introduced to all of the contestants, but for the life of her, Moira couldn't remember their names.

"I'm ready to head back to our rooms if you are," her daughter said, barely covering up a yawn. "I thought I would want to explore a bit tonight, but after all that food I'm too tired even to think about climbing stairs."

"Let's get going," Moira agreed. "I have an early

CURRIED LOBSTER MURDER

morning tomorrow, and I still want to video call David tonight."

She said a quick goodbye to Sofia, who also looked tired, then followed her daughter out the banquet hall doors and back down the hallway toward their rooms. The ship didn't move noticeably, but whatever imperceptible movement there was threw her balance off just enough that she had to put her hand on the wall for support. She was sure she would get her sea legs soon, but for now she was happy enough just to avoid falling on her face.

She was just beginning to wonder if Candice really knew the way back or if they'd taken a wrong turn somewhere when a terrified scream cut through the air. Moira and her daughter traded a look, then without a word took off in the direction of the scream, turning a corner and almost running into a curious bystander in their hurry.

The deli owner slowed to a stop when she saw the

woman kneeling in the middle of a hallway with a blood-stained figure in her arms. She recognized the lady; it was Linda, one of the women they'd shared the table with. That meant that the person in her arms must be...

"Bobby," Linda whimpered. "Bobby, sweetie, hang on. We're going to get you help."

"What happened?" Moira asked, kneeling down next to her. People were beginning to come out of their rooms to see what the commotion was about, and she could hear the sound of footsteps as more people raced down the hallway.

Bobby was taking slow, wet-sounding breaths in Linda's arms. The deli owner glanced at his body to see where he was hurt, then quickly looked away. His throat had been slit, and even she could tell by the amount of blood staining his shirt and his wife's arms that he wasn't going to make it.

"I-I found him like this," Linda sobbed. "Can you help? Please, we need to get him to a doctor."

"I don't know what I can do," the deli owner said, her voice cracking. She looked around helplessly, hoping that someone with authority would come to their aid, but there were only the shocked faces of other guests staring at them. Candice was keeping them back, futilely telling them to go get help, but no one was leaving.

"Out of my way, out of my way," a commanding voice said at last. "Let me through. What's going—"

The man broke off mid-sentence as he caught sight of the bloody man and woman in the middle of the hallway. Moira stumbled back to give him room as he crouched down and pressed his fingers against Bobby's wrist. The deli owner watched the man's chest for signs that he was still breathing—he had been just a moment ago, hadn't he? — but seconds passed with no sound or movement from him. At last the man who had taken charge sighed and stood up. He looked pale, but determined.

"Jim, get a clean sheet out of the linen closet," he snapped to one of the stewards who had been watching the scene unfold with everyone. "Help me cover this poor man. I'll page the medics and ask them to bring a stretcher."

He turned back to Linda, who was sobbing and hugging her husband's body.

"Ma'am, I'm going to need you to let go and stand up now."

"Are... are you going to help him?"

The man's lips tightened, but he nodded. "I need you to give us some space so we can get him down to the infirmary."

Bobby's wife reluctantly released her husband and got to her feet, taking a horrified step back as she realized how much blood had pooled beneath them. Jim reappeared with a stark white sheet in his hand, which the two men then used to cover the still form of the man on the floor.

"Why did you cover his face?" Linda said, her voice becoming hysterical. "He has to breathe."

She moved to grab the sheet off, but Jim wrapped an arm around her waist and pulled her back. Before the situation could escalate, two paramedics carrying a collapsible stretcher arrived and loaded the sheet-covered form onto it. Linda was sobbing by now, and the man who had taken charge of the situation approached her, speaking gently. Moira watched them, not sure what to do or how to help. She saw a door open behind the crowd that had gathered as someone else joined the mob.

"My name is Xavier Rodgers, and I'm the ship's first mate. What's your name? Was that your husband?"

She nodded tearfully. "Yes, he's my husband. My name is Linda. We have a son back home. Please... can I go to Bobby? I don't want him to be alone."

Her voice broke on the last word and she started sobbing again. Xavier took her arm and guided her down the hall where the medics had taken her husband's body.

"We'll go to him now, all right? On the way, why don't you tell me what happened?"

The deli owner listened for as long as she could while the two walked away, but Linda's distraught words were barely intelligible. Soon enough, Jim was shooing everyone away, asking them to go back to their rooms or to one of the twenty-four hour bars while the cleaning crews took care of the mess in the hallway. Moira and Candice left with the crowd, heading back to their own rooms in unspoken agreement.

"That was horrible," Candice said, taking a seat on her mother's bed once they made it back. "That poor woman... and her poor husband. What do you think happened?"

"I don't know," Moira said. "I'm sure we'll hear something about it tomorrow. I wonder if they're going to cancel the competition? It's going to be tough on everyone once they find out that one of the contestants died."

"Do they have any sort of police out here?" her daughter asked. "I don't remember seeing anything about security while we were boarding."

"I think there are some security officers, but no official police. Laws are different in international waters.

From what I've read, it doesn't seem like there will be much in the way of investigation until we get back to Miami."

"Do you think that they're going to turn the ship around? That man could have been murdered for all we know."

"I doubt it," Moira said after a moment's thought. "Somehow I don't think they're going to turn the whole cruise ship around for one person. Sadly, these sorts of things are all about money. If they can get away with it, they'll probably just sail right along as if nothing had happened. I don't know what they're going to do about his body. The ship might have a morgue, I guess."

"Do you think his wife is going to get off at the next port?" the young woman asked.

"If I were her, I would," she told her daughter.

"There's no way I would be able to finish a cruise after a loved one died like that."

They fell silent, each subdued by their own thoughts and imagining themselves in Linda's place. It was a dark beginning to their trip, and Moira hoped that it wasn't a foreshadowing of what was to come. Had she made a mistake when she entered her name into the drawing for the competition? *I want to talk to David*, she thought. *But I don't think he'll be up this late.*

"I think we should go to sleep and talk about this again in the morning," Moira said. "I'm exhausted, and I have to wake up early regardless of whether or not they're going to cancel the Chef War. We'll get breakfast early and see if we can find anything out about what happened to Bobby Babcock while we eat. I'm sure they'll tell us something when we meet for the first challenge either way."

"All right, I guess," Candice said reluctantly. "It's

going to be hard to get to sleep not knowing what's going on, but I guess we don't have any other choice. Goodnight, Mom."

With that the young woman got up and walked into her own room, closing the adjoining door behind her. The deli owner pulled off her shoes, peeled off her dress, struggled into her pajamas, and collapsed in her bed. She was tired, but she knew that Candice had been right. It was going to be hard to get to sleep with her mind racing like this. For a second she considered sending another email to David, telling him what had happened, but decided against it. He would just worry. It would be better to wait until she had more information to give him.

Tossing and turning, trying futilely to ignore the images of the dead man that kept appearing when she turned her eyes, it was a long time before she managed to fall asleep.

## CHAPTER SIX

The alarm clock bolted to her nightstand went off at six o'clock the next morning. She pulled herself out of her slumber and looked around for a moment, blinking as she took in her strange surroundings. *Where am I?* Then it all came back to her—winning the entry to the competition on the cruise, enjoying the fantastic dinner the night before, and, most of all, seeing the dead man.

She got up and walked over to the small window in her socks. Outside it was overcast, and she could see nothing but the dark ocean. It looked windier than yesterday and the waves had white crests as they raced across the water.

PATTI BENNING

She took a deep breath and rested her forehead against the cool glass. In just under two hours she had her first challenge to get through—if the Chef War hadn't been cancelled due to Bobby's death. First things first; she had to shower, get dressed, and meet her daughter for breakfast.

They met at a breakfast buffet on the cruise ship's top deck, giving them an unbeatable view of the surrounding ocean. Despite the clouds and wind, it was warm enough to eat outside comfortably, and the fresh, clean air helped to clear Moira's head.

"Before you got here, I asked a few other people if they knew what happened," her daughter said. "No one has a clue."

"I'll just have to wait until the first challenge to find out," the deli owner said. "Let's put that out of our minds for now. There's nothing we can do anyway, and we should at least try to enjoy this trip while we can. What are you going to do while I'm at the challenge?"

Each challenge would be recorded, edited, and then played for the cruise guests later that evening. The show wouldn't be available on national television, but the thought of over a thousand people seeing her possibly making a fool of herself in the competition was nerve wracking. During the hours of the competition, Candice would be on her own to enjoy the cruise and take advantage of their all-expenses paid vacation. Moira would have to make do with sneaking a few hours at the spa after the stress of each challenge. Assuming, of course, she didn't get disqualified after the first one.

"I thought I would check out some of the restaurants and take a look at the theater. I heard that it has a pool in it, so you can swim while a movie is playing," the young woman said. "Then after the challenge we can meet at one of the nicer restaurants for lunch."

"Sounds good." She smiled, but when she looked down at the food on her plate, her stomach clenched. She was too nervous to eat. It was all she could do to get her coffee down and pick at her bacon while happy couples on the cruise chatted around them.

The first challenge was being held in the industrial kitchen next to the beautiful banquet hall they'd dined in last night. With Bobby out of the picture, Moira was now one of six contestants, and the other five were huddled nervously in a group when she came in. Sofia gave her a quick smile and beckoned her over.

"We're just waiting for the judges," she said. "I was beginning to wonder if something had happened to you too. I just heard about Mr. Babcock... how horrible. He was at your table, wasn't he?"

"Yes," Moira said. "He was." She noticed that four of

the other contestants watched her expectantly; the fifth, Nadine, just looked pale.

"They've been asking me questions about him for the past ten minutes," she said. "I keep telling them I didn't know him that well..."

"Word is he killed himself," another contestant, a man named Antonio Cross, said. "Did he seem depressed to you? Did he say anything to make you think, in retrospect, that he was planning this?"

"Whoa," Moira said, raising her hands. "I barely knew the guy. We talked for a couple of hours, mostly about food. He seemed pretty normal, I guess. That was it. If anything, he seemed like a happy guy."

"You were there, weren't you? When he died?" a woman asked. The deli owner couldn't remember her name.

"Yes, I was. My daughter and I heard his wife scream and thought we should see what was happening. I didn't see it happen, but I saw them afterward. It was... it was terrible."

The room fell silent for a moment as the contestants digested this.

"Do you think she did it?" Antonio asked. "His wife, I mean? I know some people said it was suicide, but that just seems like a convenient explanation. What if he was murdered, and they just don't want to shut the competition down so they're keeping it quiet?"

"I've got no idea," she told him. "But she seemed really distraught. I guess she could just be a good actor, but it really seemed like she loved him."

She frowned, not liking the way the conversation

was going. She didn't want to keep going over and over the man's death. It was a terrible thing to think about, and discussing it again wouldn't help anything.

Luckily, before anyone else could ask another question, the door to the kitchen opened and Damien Warner walked in, followed closely by Charlie, who looked as bright and alert as ever.

"It looks like everyone's here," he said with a quick count of the six of them. "We're going to get started on the challenge soon, but first there is an important issue that I'll let Charlie address while I double-check your stations."

Charlie stepped forward, clipboard in hand. "As some of you may have heard, last night we suffered a terrible loss. One of our contestants, Bobby Babcock, killed himself."

The six remaining contestants fell silent. *Suicide? It that really the official explanation?* Moira thought. *I don't believe it. He had so much hope for this competition. Why would he end his life before it even began?*

"What happened?" Antonio asked. "How did he do it? All we heard was that there was a lot of blood."

"He slit his throat with a razor," she told him. "We've obviously never had anything like this happen before, and while we debated whether or not to put a hold on the competition, we decided to go ahead. Though he was a contestant, we do not feel that his death had anything to do with the Chef War, and it wouldn't be right to let his personal issues take precedence over everyone else's enjoyment of the cruise. If no one else has any questions, I would like to—"

Antonio cut her off, asking, "What about his wife? Is she going to get off the cruise early?"

"While Mrs. Babcock is free to stay and enjoy the rest of the cruise courtesy of Mr. Warner, I believe she is planning on departing along with her husband's body at our first stop in Labadee, Haiti."

"See?" Antonio whispered, edging closer to Moira. "She could have killed him. Most crimes on cruise ships go unsolved. I bet you she's going to have him cremated when she gets back, and that will be that. No investigation, just a death certificate and an urn."

"I don't think she killed him," Moira replied in a low voice. "You didn't see her; she was distraught."

She could tell the man was still skeptical, but Charlie spoke again before he could get another word in. "I would like to take a moment of silence for Mr. Babcock before we begin the first challenge."

She bowed her head, and Moira and the other

contestants followed suit. The room fell silent until Charlie cleared her throat a few minutes later.

"I think it is time to finally begin your first challenge. Damien will explain the rules, and I will be available to answer any questions that arise. Once the challenge begins, you will have forty-five minutes to complete it. A camera crew will be joining us shortly—please ignore them. Remember the footage will be edited before it's available to the other guests on the cruise. The videos will be available online a few days after the competition ends, and contestants will get a DVD mailed to them at the address you provided when you signed up."

By the time she had finished speaking, Damien had reappeared. He thanked Charlie, then beckoned the contestants over.

"You each have a station with all of the tools you should need to complete this first challenge. Once the timer starts, we ask that you stay out of each other's stations. That way there can't be any complaints of cheating or interfering, not that I think any of you wonderful people would do anything like that. The fridge, cupboard, and spice racks are all fully stocked, and there should be more than enough of all the ingredients to go around. If for some reason there isn't, just let Charlie know and she will make sure more is brought down from one of the other kitchens. Will everyone please approach their stations now?"

Moira and the other contestants shuffled nervously to their stations in the huge, stainless steel filled kitchen. She was already feeling intimidated by the shiny new appliances, which were both better and bigger than what she had in the deli. At least the basic tools at her station—the knife, the cutting board, the measuring cups, and mixing bowls—were all similar to what she was used to.

"Each of you should have a laminated pamphlet at your station with the specific rules for this challenge. Does everybody see theirs?" All six of them nodded.

"Good. As you can see, the first challenge is a break-fast dish with a twist. You cannot use eggs, bacon, sausage, waffles, or pancakes during this challenge. Whoever comes up with the most creative and tasty dish, to be judged by Felicity, Walter, and myself, wins. We will be ranking you from one to six, and whoever comes in sixth place will be disqualified—though, of course, you are still free to enjoy every-thing else this cruise has to offer. Any questions?"

No one spoke up, though Moira's mind was swirling with them. Was that it? No more directions... she just had to make a breakfast dish without using any of the most common ingredients. *Easy*, she thought, beginning to panic. *I'll just whip something up that I've never made before and hope it tastes good enough to win the competition... what could go wrong?*

# CHAPTER SEVEN

The moment the timer rang signaling the beginning of the challenge, the deli owner burst into action. She had no idea what she was going to make yet, but she didn't want to be the only one left standing clueless at her station. She decided to look through the pantry until she saw something that sparked an idea in her, and go from there.

Damien Warner had left the kitchen before the timer had gone off, leaving only Charlie to supervise. Well, Charlie and the three cameramen, who seemed determined not to miss a thing. At first, Moira had been certain that she wouldn't be able to focus on anything but the cameras filming her every move; to her surprise, the instant the competition started, they stopped mattering.

She pulled open the pantry and raked her eyes over the shelves, desperate for something to inspire her. Should she try to make muffins from scratch? Baking had never been her strong suit; it probably wouldn't be a good idea to pin the competition on her ability to create a delicious muffin recipe on her first try. The deli owner bit back a groan, wishing her mind wasn't so blank. Maybe it was the lack of sleep, or the thoughts of Bobby's death the night before, but she just couldn't seem to concentrate on food. She was just about to close the pantry doors and go check the fridge when her eyes fell on a container of oats. *Should I make oatmeal?* she thought.

Suddenly she remembered something, one of her favorite things about visiting her grandmother when she was younger—banana oatmeal breakfast cookies. They were delicious, didn't include any of the ingredients that had been banned for this challenge and, best of all, she even had a pretty good idea of how to make them. *I may be able to win this thing after all,* she thought, reaching for the can of oats. *Or at least not get disqualified during the first round.*

She gathered a few other ingredients, then returned to her station, stealing a few surreptitious glances toward what the other contestants were working on. Sofia was making some sort of breakfast biscuit, and Nadine was doing something with fruit. Would her breakfast cookies stand a chance against everyone else's food? She didn't know, but now that she was back at her station with all of her ingredients, she was committed.

She started by preheating the oven and pulling the largest mixing bowl off the rack. After giving her hands a good wash, she measured out the oats. She added a pinch of salt and a dash of cinnamon, then set to peeling and mashing the bananas, her eyes on the clock. Once the bananas were in, she returned to the pantry and grabbed a jar of almond butter, scooped a cup of it into the mixing bowl, poured in as much pure maple syrup as she dared and, after a moment's hesitation, visited the pantry once more for a small bag of chocolate chips. The judges wanted something creative and tasty; they were going to get it.

She mixed the dough with her hands just as her grandmother had done, then spooned it onto a cookie sheet in small dollops. She then slid the sheet into the oven and set the timer for fifteen minutes, though she would check on the cookies after ten. *I'm just guessing on the time*, she thought nervously as she began to clean up. *But then, I was guessing on pretty much everything else as well. Did my grandmother use maple syrup or honey? I can't remember. Too bad we weren't allowed to use eggs... I probably could have whipped up a prize-winning quiche in a heartbeat—I do make them a couple of times every week at the deli.*

She spent the next fifteen minutes cleaning up her station and peering nervously at the breakfast cookies. The kitchen was filling up with delicious scents of cooking food, but she was too nervous to enjoy it. A cameraman stopped by her station. He panned the lens over her clean cooking station, then crouched down to film through the oven window where the cookies were nearly done. Moira gave the camera an anxious smile as it swept over her face. She tried to examine the cameraman's expression to see if he had any opinions on the dish that she had come up with, but his face was impassive.

The wait was the worst part. She was relieved when she opened the oven a third time to check on the cookies and they finally looked done. She had only a few minutes to spare, so she quickly took the cookie sheet out, grabbed the three plates for the judges, and waited for them to cool for as long as she could before transferring two cookies to each plate. The other contestants were all hurrying as well, and there was the sound of breaking glass and a quiet curse as someone dropped something a few stations to her right.

The deli owner put down her spatula just as the bell rang to signal the end of the competition and looked around. Everyone else looked like they had at least finished putting their food on the plates for the judges. One woman—was it Daphne? —was nursing a burnt hand, and several people looked to be on the verge of tears.

"All right," Charlie said. "Everyone wash up and then follow me. Leave the plates for the judges where they are; they'll be brought in separately."

Moira and the six other contestants followed her out of the kitchen and into the banquet hall where they had eaten the night before. The long table was still up on the stage, but instead of small round tables on the floor below, there were simply six chairs lined up facing the judges. The contestants filed slowly down the line, each of them taking a seat with nervous glances around. The deli owner felt exposed, which she realized must be the point. There was nothing— no table, no counter—between the contestants and the judges. Nothing to shield them from any harsh words they had about the dishes, and nothing to hide reactions from the cameras. She gulped. This couldn't be over with quickly enough.

"Congratulations! You all made it through the first part of your first challenge," Damien Warner said from his seat at the center of the long table up on the stage. "Now all you have to do is sit back and relax while we do the rest of the work. Charlie will call each of your names as we bring your dish out. When you hear your name, I expect you to rise and approach the table while we taste your dish. Then each judge will tell you what he or she liked or disliked about the dish, and you will be asked to return to your seat. You won't be getting your scores until all of the dishes have been tasted. Any questions? No? Then let's begin."

Antonio was called forward first. He had made hash browns topped with shredded chicken, onions, corn, beans, cheese, and a homemade hot sauce. The judges were silent as they tasted the food. Moira could see Antonio shift his weight nervously as the three judges chewed. She bit her lip, knowing that she would get her own chance in the spotlight soon enough— not looking forward to it at all.

"It looks like you followed the rules to a T." Damien said, putting his fork down at last. "Before we tell you what we think of your dish, would you mind telling us what inspired it?"

"Well, I'm allergic to a lot of things," the man began. "Peanuts, shellfish, eggs... the list goes on. That means I'm used to cooking with limitations, and at my restaurant we offer a lot of limited ingredient dishes so people with allergies or food sensitivities can enjoy good cooking too. This is actually pretty similar to one of our most popular breakfast dishes, I just substituted chicken for the bacon that I usually use. It's a hearty dish to get you going in the morning and keep you satisfied until lunch time."

"Impressive. I love seeing our contestants using their own strengths to their advantage during this competition. The whole idea is to make you all better cooks in the end." The head judge beamed at them, then turned his attention back to Antonio. "As for this dish, I appreciate the variety of textures—I love how the corn kernels just pop between my teeth—but the hash browns seem a bit underdone."

"Sorry," the cook said. "I actually started making something else, and changed my mind partway through. I know the hash browns didn't get enough time in the pan."

Damien just nodded in acknowledgment, then inclined his head toward Felicity, who was sitting on his right.

"I'd just like to say that I absolutely love this hot sauce," she said. "I need the recipe when this is all done. However, I have to second Damien on the hash browns—they are a bit too soggy for my taste— and I would also like to add that you should work on your presentation. While the food tastes good, the way it's just scooped haphazardly onto the plate like this makes it look like something a cat hacked up."

Antonio's lips tightened and he lowered his gaze before turning to face Walter, the last judge to speak.

"I thought the hash browns were fine," the last judge said. "I don't like them too crispy. My main complaint is the lack of flavor. Other than the hot sauce, you really didn't use any other spices. This dish would be much better with some garlic, and maybe a dash of sage or even fresh cilantro on top. You don't want every bite to taste exactly the same in a breakfast skillet like this."

"Thank you, that's good advice," Antonio said. "I'll keep all of it in mind for next time."

The deli owner saw him take a deep breath as he returned to his seat. *That didn't go too poorly,* she thought. *It could have been worse. Good for him.*

She listened keenly as the next few people before her went. The judges weren't too harsh with any of them, which was a relief. Moira had been dreading the sort of experience that she had seen on some of her favorite cooking shows, where the judges ripped the contestants apart with their words and sent them home in tears.

At last it was her turn. Damien called her up and asked her what ingredients had gone into the breakfast cookies. She told him, then waited anxiously while he bit into one. A thousand fears rushed through her mind. *Were they cooked well enough? Had she used too much syrup? Did the chocolate chips make the cookies too sweet?* Then, at last, her time for worrying was over and the head judge was speaking.

"Very impressive, Ms. Darling. I love the blend of flavors, and the consistency of the cookies is just perfect. May I ask what inspired this recipe? Is it something that you normally serve at your deli?"

"No, sir," she said. "My grandmother actually used to make these, or something similar. It's an old family recipe."

*If they really are that good, I just may have to start offering them at the deli along with the quiches,* she thought. *With a few tweaks in the recipe, we could have a few different varieties—one for each day of the week, maybe.* Her train of thought was put on hold when Damien started speaking again.

"Well it's quite tasty and meets all of the requirements for the challenge, however I do think the cookies are a bit on the sweet side. They're more like something you would serve as a dessert after dinner than something to start off your day. I would suggest dialing down the sugar content a bit and perhaps adding something tart, like dried blueberries or cranberries, to even out the flavor. I enjoy the chocolate chips, but I think the recipe would be even better with about half of what you put in."

She suppressed a spike of annoyance at herself for adding so many sweet ingredients and tried to focus on the positive; Damien's review of her breakfast cookies wasn't bad at all compared to what he had told a few of the contestants. She held her breath as Felicity began to speak, and it wasn't until Walter had finished his turn by saying that the cookies were overall very good, though he thought peanut butter would have been a better choice to go with the chocolate and banana flavors, that she let herself relax. She doubted that she had won the challenge, but the judges seemed to like her food more than some of the other dishes that they had tasted.

Feeling almost giddy with relief, she returned to her seat while the judges finished with the last two contestants. When it was finally time for their scores, she felt herself tense up again. In just a few minutes, one of their numbers would be banned from the competition. The only question was, who?

# CHAPTER EIGHT

"We will start by announcing the winner," Damien said after a moment of conferring with his fellow judges. "Daphne, your fruit and granola bowl with the maple icing was as close to a perfect dish as I've ever had. It was unique, and really showed your creative side. I'm happy to announce that by unanimous vote, we have decided to give you first place in this challenge. This means that you'll be exempt from disqualification in the next challenge, and I look forward to seeing your creativity really shine tomorrow."

He smiled and the rest of them politely clapped as a tearful Daphne stammered her thanks and approached to shake the judge's hands. She returned to the line of contestants and the judges moved on to congratulating the person who got second place: Sofia.

"Third place we have Moira Darling and her tasty breakfast cookies. You can't go wrong with those, especially if you've got a sweet tooth."

Stunned, it took the deli owner a moment to get her feet moving. She beamed at the judges as she shook their hands, and couldn't keep from smiling even after she returned to the other contestants. Third out of six may not have been the best score possible, but it definitely wasn't bad. She couldn't wait to tell David and her employees at the deli about today's challenge.

Nadine got fourth place, and the judges moved on until only one was left. Antonio Cross accepted his disqualification with lips pressed thinly together and an angry glint in his eye.

"We'll be sorry to see you go, Antonio," Damien said gravely. "Remember that this in no way means you are a bad cook. You have a successful business, and I'm sure you will keep on succeeding where it counts. Feel free to enjoy the rest of the now stress-free cruise, and be sure to keep up with the competition as the videos are released each night. I'm sure you'll want to see how your fellow contestants are doing."

"Screw this." Antonio stormed out of the room. The other contestants were quiet for only a moment before congratulating each other, each of them happy not to have been disqualified. Moira and Sofia exchanged a quick hug, and Nadine beamed at them both.

"I'm so glad I made it," she said to them. "I hardly slept last night, I was so worried about today."

"Me too," Sofia said. "I know the chances of me winning aren't very high—I think I'm the least experienced out of all of us—but I could really use that money."

"We all could, I think," said Nadine. "Ten grand is a lot. We all got lucky—I'm sure it was a very hard decision for the judges. None of us is bad at what we do. This is going to be a close competition."

"I'm envious of Daphne," Moira admitted. "For the next challenge, she won't have the stress of worrying that she'll get disqualified, so I bet she'll do even better."

"Ugh, that's not fair," Sofia groaned. "They should let the person who came in second to last have immunity, since they obviously need the help. I wish they would tell us what we're going to be making ahead of time so we can plan our dishes—that would help me a lot."

The deli owner and Nadine both agreed with her.

*Maybe they will for the next challenge*, Moira thought. *Maybe they only wanted us to think on our feet for the first one.* However, when Damien spoke again, she realized they would have no such luck.

"Congratulations to the five of you," he told them after standing up to get their attention. "You've all made it to the next round. The second challenge will take place tomorrow at eleven. You will report to the same kitchen that you did today where Charlie will give you further instructions. Until then, enjoy the cruise and feel free to catch the footage of this morning's challenge on the ship's television network tonight after dinner. Good luck to all of you. I look forward to trying the food that you prepare for tomorrow's challenge!"

With that, they were dismissed. Moira followed Sofia out of the banquet hall, still floating on the feeling of placing third. She had a whole day before she had to worry about the next challenge, and looked like it was time to catch up with David and her crew at the deli at last.

She met Candice on her way back to her room. Her daughter was eager to hear what had happened, so she gave her a quick rundown of the challenge, adding that an edited version would be playing on the cruise ship's closed circuit TVs that evening.

"What did you do with your morning?" she asked the young woman as she unlocked her door.

"I spent most of it at the pool," Candice told her. "The sky cleared up, and the water was just perfect. It was just amazing. Everyone's in such a good mood, the food and drinks are amazing—and free—and the air is so fresh. Will you have any time to relax at all while we're here?"

"Well, I don't have anything else I have to do for the challenge until tomorrow at eleven. I was going to check my computer and try video calling David, after that we can hit the pool together if you want."

"Sounds great," her daughter told her with a grin. "I'm going to go rest in my room for a bit—all of this sun made me tired—so just knock on my door when you're ready to go out."

With that, Candice disappeared into her own room and Moira shut the connecting door behind her and sat down at her desk. She pressed the space bar on the detachable keyboard to wake her tablet up, then pulled up her email. There was one from the deli's email address, and one from David. She opened the deli's first.

*Hey Ms. D,*

*I just wanted to let you know that everything is going well here. All of us wish you luck and hope you're kicking butt at the competition. We can't wait to hear how it's going!*

*-Allison*

The deli owner smiled and replied with a quick message telling them that she had gotten third place in the first competition, and might have come up with a new option for their breakfast menu. She ended the email by saying she had high hopes for the rest of the competition, thanked them for their support, and promised to keep them updated. Next, she opened David's message.

*Moira,*

*The dogs are doing well, though they seem to miss you. Maverick kept running up to your room this morning and wouldn't eat breakfast until I let him in and showed him you weren't there. Keeva keeps watching out the window —I think she expects you to show up at any moment. I took them out on a walk after breakfast, and plan on letting them spend the day at the office with me. I think my clients will love them.*

*I'm glad to hear that everything has gone well for you so far. Don't worry about the ship. Those things are pretty safe these days, and as long as you pay attention during the safety drills and remember where the life jackets and lifeboats are, you'll be perfectly fine even if something does go wrong. It's not like the* Titanic—*modern ships have enough emergency equipment for everyone.*

*By the time you read this, you'll probably have started the competition. I would wish you luck, but I know you don't need it. I can't wait to hear all about it.*

*With love,*

*David (and two very spoiled pooches)*

Moira started to reply, then decided to try giving him a video call instead. He would probably be at his office by now, which meant that as long as he wasn't with a client, he would be at his desk with his open laptop in front of him.

Sure enough, he answered the call right away. The deli owner adjusted her tablet's screen until the camera was at a good angle, then did her best to ignore the small screen showing her own face in the lower corner. Instead, she looked at David and smiled.

"I was wondering when I'd hear from you," he said with a grin. His voice was only slightly distorted by the wireless connection and the tablet's cheap speakers, and the video quality was surprisingly good. "How's everything going?"

"Great," Moira told him, still giddy with her high score in the first challenge. When she remembered the dead man, she sobered.

"Well, I placed high in the competition," she amended. "I'll get to that soon, but something else happened that you're probably going to want to hear about."

"What happened? Are you and Candice okay?" He leaned forward, his voice now full of concern.

"Yes, we're both fine, but one of the other contestants isn't. In fact, he's dead."

She told David everything she knew about Bobby Babcock, starting with the dinner she had with him on the first night to witnessing his final moments in the hallway. She told him about the conjectures of the other contestants, and what Charlie had told them about the man's death being suicide.

"And what do you think?" David asked when she was done. "You were there, and I trust your judgment more than that of someone I've never met."

The deli owner hesitated, knowing that what she was about to say would only concern David more, but not willing to lie to him even to spare him worry.

"I don't think he killed himself," she said at last. "But I also don't think his wife killed him. The way she was acting... I don't think anyone could fake that kind of emotion. She was hysterical."

"What makes you say it wasn't suicide?" he asked. "Not that I disagree, I just want to hear your reasoning."

"Well, at dinner he seemed like he was really looking forward to the competition. He seemed to think that he had a pretty good chance of winning and, well, he seemed happy. I know that I'm basing all of this on a couple hours' worth of conversation. He could have had a lot going on that I don't know about, but it really just doesn't make sense to me that he would have killed himself before the competition had even started."

"I agree with you. Do you think it could have been one of the other contestants?"

"I honestly don't know," she said with a sigh. "Like I said, the competition hadn't even started yet. He hadn't won anything; we hadn't even seen him cook. Why would anyone take that kind of risk before even knowing if someone was going to be a threat or not? Why would anyone take that kind of risk at all? Ten thousand dollars doesn't seem like enough to risk going to jail over."

"People have killed for less," he told her. She sighed.

"Let's talk about something else," she said. "Are the dogs there? How are they doing?"

He turned his computer so she could see the German shepherd and Irish wolfhound lying peacefully in front of his desk. Moira smiled, glad that they seemed so happy. He turned the screen back to himself and asked her how the first challenge had gone. Feeling the excitement bubble up in her again, the deli owner began rehashing the events of the morning with him, glad that she had someone so special to her to share these once-in-a-lifetime moments with.

# CHAPTER NINE

After ending her phone call with David, Moira took
a relaxing shower, relishing in the endless hot water
on the cruise ship, then put her swimsuit on. She
pulled a cover-up over her shoulders, slipped her
feet into her sandals, grabbed her room card, then
knocked on Candice's door. It was time to start
having some fun on this cruise, and push thoughts
of the murder and the competition out of her mind,
for the time being at least.

It was hot out, much hotter than she was expecting.
*Of course, we're further south now,* she thought. *Way
past Florida. I bet it will get even warmer as we keep
moving down into the Caribbean.* It was a pleasant
change from the chilly Michigan weather that she

had been tolerating back at home for the past few weeks, and she couldn't wait to set her sights on the first tropical beach.

The pool that Candice led them to was absolutely gorgeous. The water was crystal clear and looked inviting, and there were fountains around the edges. The pool was lined with reclining lounges and round tables with umbrellas over them so people could catch some shade if they got tired of sunbathing. There was a drink bar at one end, and one of the restaurants a little bit farther away had live music playing.

"This has got to be one of the best vacations ever," she told her daughter as they each grabbed a towel and settled themselves onto a pair of reclining chairs. "I don't think I've ever even seen a pool with fountains anywhere other than on TV."

"Thanks again for inviting me to go on this cruise," Candice said. "Though of course it would have been fine if you had invited David. I have to admit, I kind of wonder why you *didn't* invite him."

"I thought about it," Moira admitted. "But I figured that as long as things keep going well between us, we have years ahead of us to spend time together. But you... you're going to have more and more things to keep you busy as time goes on. Who knows, in a few years you could be married, you could even have kids. You might move to another city, or another state, or even another country if that's what you want. I wanted to take this time together while we can, because I know that it won't be as easy once you have a family of your own."

"Aww, Mom, that's so sweet. Don't worry, though, I don't plan on moving to another country any time soon. Or having kids. I've got a career to build first, after all."

"From what you've told me, you're doing a great job of that." The deli owner smiled over at her daughter, then glanced at the pool. "I think I'm going to take a dip to cool off, then catch some sun for a while. Martha and Denise are going to be jealous when I come back home with a tan in the middle of fall."

Just as Candice had promised, the water was perfect; cool enough to help wash away the heat of the sun, but not so cold that she was reluctant to go in. She realized that being disqualified from the competition might not be so bad after all—the people who got disqualified early on would have the entire rest of the cruise to do whatever they wanted, something that was probably a rare occurrence for all of them. She knew firsthand how much work it took to run a restaurant. *Of course, I'm still going to try my hardest to win*, she thought, resting her elbows on the side of the pool and gazing out through the ship's railing at the endless sea beyond. *That cooking segment would be amazing, not to mention how nice the $10,000 would be. Think of everything I could buy for the deli!*

She sighed and closed her eyes, feeling truly peaceful for the first time since boarding the cruise ship. Whether she won or lost, she was going to have fun and enjoy herself. *I hope Antonio doesn't feel too bad about being disqualified,* she thought idly. *He looked pretty upset. I hope he ends up enjoying the rest of the cruise.*

It was well into the evening by the time she and Candice decided they'd had enough of the pool. All the free drinks in the world couldn't curb the hunger that had begun gnawing at her. She had skipped lunch, being too excited about her good score in the competition to even think about it, and now that it was almost dinner, she was ravenous.

The cruise ship had countless places to eat, from buffet halls, to formal dining experiences, to chain restaurants with tropical themes. They decided to try out the dining hall that they had been assigned to when they first came on board. After a quick stop at their rooms to change, they found their way to the right room and were seated by a friendly maître d' who left them with menus that presented their options for the four course meal. A few moments later they were joined by Daphne, her boyfriend, and the other contestant, a man named Hector.

"What did you think of the first challenge?" Hector asked once introductions had been made all around. "Breakfast isn't really my strong suit. The pub that I work at doesn't open until two."

"I enjoyed it," Daphne said. "I work best under pressure. The time limit and ingredient limitations really forced me to think, and it let me forget about the cameras and the high stakes."

"It wasn't as bad as I was expecting," Moira told them. "Maybe I watch too many cooking shows, but I was thinking it would be a lot more intense. The judges are actually pretty nice, and even when they were telling us what we could improve on, they weren't rude."

"And the contestants too... it's nothing like what you would think. No one had been rude at all," Daphne said. "Well, Antonio was a bit grumpy when I ran into him earlier. But I had lunch with a few other contestants, and everyone was perfectly nice."

"I think most of the drama on reality TV cooking shows is scripted," Hector said. "Normal people just don't act like that."

"I don't know," the deli owner said. "In my experience, people can be pretty petty. I wouldn't be surprised if people begin losing their tempers once things start to heat up in the competition."

"You may be right," Daphne said. "But personally, I don't think any contest is worth losing your basic human decency over."

The waiter appeared with their first course: salad for Candice and Hector, a bowl of clam chowder for Moira, and a seafood appetizer platter for Daphne and her boyfriend. With music playing in the background and the friendly chatter of other guests around her, the five of them dug in.

Their meal was interrupted a moment later when Daphne rose suddenly from the table, her hand clamped over her mouth.

"I feel sick," she blurted out before rushing from the table. Her boyfriend followed quickly after her. Moira, Candice, and Hector all exchanged glances.

"I hope she's all right," Candice said.

"Me too." Hector paused, then sheepishly added, "Though I wouldn't really mind if she felt too sick to take part in the second challenge tomorrow. I'd hope that she got better right after, of course."

"Don't say that; the poor woman would be crushed if she missed out on the next challenge," Moira said, trying to take the high road. But she couldn't help thinking that if Daphne was too sick to compete tomorrow then maybe, just maybe, she might have a better chance of winning herself. The other woman had already proven herself to be a good cook... without her in the competition, might Moira have a shot at winning this round?

# CHAPTER TEN

"Yesterday we told you what ingredients you had to avoid," Charlie began once all five of the contestants still in the running were gathered in the kitchen the next day. "Today, we're going to give you a list of ingredients that you *have* to use. What you make with them is up to you, and you are free to use any additional ingredients that you want, but forgetting even one of the required ingredients is grounds for instant disqualification. The list of ingredients is next to each of your stations. Once again, you will have forty-five minutes to complete the dish. I'll be walking around just like last time, so if you have any questions, feel free to give me a shout. Is everyone ready?"

She beamed at them, sweeping her gaze across the room to make sure no one looked confused before giving a satisfied nod and reaching over to start the timer. The buzzer rang, and the five of them ran to their stations to get started.

Moira grabbed the ingredient list and began reading:

*Bok choy*

*Lobster*

*Carrots*

*Curry powder*

*Red dates*

*Candied ginger*

The candied ginger made her think of Candice and her homemade candies; she smiled briefly, then the reality hit her. She had to make a dish, in forty-five minutes, including all of these ingredients. Not only did the dish have to be palatable, it had to be better than everyone else's dish. *Or at least better than one other person's dish, if I don't want to get disqualified,* she corrected herself. Still it was going to be a challenge, and she could only hope that she was up to it.

The required ingredients were already set up at her station, but staring at them didn't spark any brilliant ideas. Should she make some sort of lobster dish over rice? Or maybe some sort of... curry pasta? None of that sounded right to her. Then her eyes landed on one of the big pots hanging above the stove, and she smiled. The answer was obvious. She was going to do what she did best; make soup.

She was keenly aware of the time limit. Somehow,

she had already wasted four of her forty-five minutes. She rushed to gather the other ingredients that she needed for the brand-new soup recipe that was forming in her mind.

First things first, she measured out some water and set it to boil in the big pot on the stove. While that heated, she began sautéing the lobster meat and bok choy in butter. Once the lobster meat and bok choy looked ready, she turned her attention to the other ingredients. The curry powder was easy; it would be the base flavor of the soup. The red dates and candied ginger were going to be her most difficult ingredients. Both were sweet, and weren't ingredients that she had ever attempted to use before in a soup. *At least lobster meat goes well with sweeter flavors,* she thought. *As long as I balance everything correctly and there's enough time to cook it, the soup shouldn't be too bad.*

She cored the dates and sliced them into quarters, then tossed them into the pot of water so they could begin cooking. The carrots she chopped into small pieces and added them as well, then added some chicken bouillon and a scoop of curry powder. The soup was already beginning to smell good. The only question was; would it be good enough to win?

The candied ginger was already thinly sliced. She began by rinsing it in cool water to remove the excess sugar, then simmered it in a shallow pan of water to begin softening it. Hopefully some of the sweetness would be drawn out while it simmered, and when she added the ginger to the soup it wouldn't affect it as much.

The clock was ticking, and she got everything in at the nick of time. *I don't know if the carrots will finish cooking,* she thought anxiously. *But there's not much I can do about that. I just need to grab a few more ingredients, and then I can let it simmer and begin cleaning up the station.*

She ended up adding onions, a few spices in addition to the curry, and cubed tofu, which she thought tied the dish together well. After double-checking the list of required ingredients to make sure she had used everything—she had—she began cleaning up the workstation. Although a cleaning crew was supposed to come through later and do it, she had always hated leaving a mess behind, and cleaning gave her something to do besides stare anxiously at her soup for the next fifteen minutes.

On her way to throw out the debris from her cutting board, she passed by the station that Daphne had been assigned to. She was shocked to see that the woman wasn't even there, and a dried-out lobster tail was sitting on the stove. Concerned, she looked around for the other woman. She knew Daphne hadn't felt well, but Moira was still surprised to see her missing from the competition completely. *It must really be serious*, she thought. *I wonder if she ate something bad? Maybe something was wrong with that seafood platter she had at the beginning of dinner last night. I wonder if her husband is sick too?* Worried, the deli owner returned to her station and began preparing the bowls for the judges.

Daphne still hadn't returned by the time the buzzer rang and the four contestants were herded into the banquet hall for the second portion of the challenge to begin. Moira overheard a couple of the others talking about Daphne, but no one seemed to know where she was. Charlie was already up on the stage talking to the judges, so it was too late to ask her. *I'll just have to wait until after they've judged the dishes to find out,* the deli owner thought. *I hope she's all right.*

Nadine was called up first. Moira gave her a supportive smile, which the other woman hesitantly returned. She saw her brace her shoulders and take a deep breath before she faced the judges.

"Nadine Jenkins, your lobster over rice was quite good," Damien said. "Well, the rice was quite good— I love how you fried it with the curry, carrots, bok choy, and dates. The lobster was unexceptional, and the sweet ginger sauce you made just didn't seem to go well with the rest of the meal."

PATTI BENNING

Nadine's shoulders fell, but she turned gamely to Felicity, who for the most part agreed with Damien.

"I would have liked to see the lobster tail flavored with curry as well as the rice," she said. "It would have tied the dish together. What you have now tastes like two separate dishes, and that just isn't working for me."

"I don't like the ginger sauce either," Walter said when it was his turn. "It tastes like it should be a salad dressing. Lobster is a flexible ingredient, but you do need to have the knowledge to pair it right."

Defeated, the woman returned to her seat. Moira saw a tear glimmer in the corner of her eye, and felt her heart ache for the poor woman. So what if she was a competitor? She was still a human being, and the deli owner didn't like to see anyone upset.

Hector went next, and his dish—he had gone with

118

pasta—was received much more positively than Nadine's had been. For a moment, Moira wondered if she should have done something with pasta or rice too. Had anyone else even made soup? She didn't remember seeing any other pots steaming on any of the stoves, but she might just have been too focused on her own cooking to pay attention to what everyone else was doing.

When Hector went back to his seat with a relieved look on his face, the five of them turned their attention to the judges to see who would be called up next. Damien took a sip of water, cleared his throat, then spoke.

"Moira Darling."

# CHAPTER ELEVEN

Moira took a deep breath and then faced the judges, unsure of what to expect. She didn't feel as confident about the soup as she had about the breakfast cookies. At least the cookies had been based on a recipe that she knew was good; the soup was a completely new recipe that she had invented on the fly.

"Delicious," Damien said, sounding almost surprised after tasting the first spoonful of soup. "The flavors blend together perfectly. Tell me, what made you think to try a soup?"

"Well, my deli serves hot soup daily, among other things," she told him. "I try to come up with new recipes as often as possible. Soup is what I'm most comfortable making, I suppose. It's kind of what I default to when I want to use a bunch of odd ingredients."

"Well in this case, it worked," he said, evidently impressed. "The only complaint I have is the tofu. It's still a bit chewy."

"I don't even like curry," Felicity added. "And even I think this is pretty good. You go, girl."

Moira beamed at her, then turned her attention to Walter.

"The tofu is chewy, and the lobster is also somewhat tough," he told her. "But other than that, it is an impressive dish. I think it's definitely the most creative out of what we've seen today."

The deli owner floated back to her seat, hardly noticing the next name being called. They had liked her soup! It seemed that the decision to go with her gut and play by her strengths had been a good one.

"It's time to give you your scores," Damien said once they had finished tasting the last contestant's dish. "This time, we will start with the lowest score. Nadine, I'm sorry, but your lobster over rice dish just did not match up with the others."

Nadine's breath hitched and she brought her hand to her mouth. Moira could imagine her holding back tears, and felt a small stab of guilt for her own success with the soup. If she had decided to make something else, she very well might have been in the other woman's place right then.

Damien then turned to Hector, who had come in second to last. Each time he addressed a new contestant, her heart beat faster until she was the only one left.

"Moira, I'm happy to announce that you're the winner of this round. Your soup was phenomenal. Congratulations, you have immunity for the next round."

He cleared his throat and looked at the other contestants. "There is an unexpected issue this round. Daphne, the winner of the last challenge, is dropping out of the competition due to a severe and unexpected illness. Since Nadine scored lowest of the contestants that actually competed this round, she would normally be disqualified, but we really can't lose two more players this early in the competition without unbalancing it, so Nadine... you got lucky. You're in it for another challenge, maybe even longer if you can come back from this."

"Thank you so much," she gasped. "I won't let you down again, I promise."

With that they were dismissed, with another day before their next challenge. Moira, still stunned by her victory, made her way back to her room and collapsed on her bed. She had done it. She had won one of the challenges. All of a sudden winning the whole competition didn't seem so far-fetched. If she kept this up, there was no reason she couldn't be the top chef in the Chef War.

With no idea where her daughter was and no way to call her without a working cell phone, Moira couldn't tell Candice the good news. She was itching to tell *someone* so she got on her tablet and opened her email. Who to tell first? If she did somehow manage to win, the prizes would affect everyone at the deli. On the other hand, it wouldn't feel right to tell her employees about her victory before even telling the man that she loved.

Decision made, she opened up a new email and was about to start typing when her tablet made a beeping noise and a pop-up informed her that a video call was incoming. She clicked the button to accept it, thinking it was David. She was surprised to see Martha and Denise peering into the camera instead.

"My goodness, you guys," she said. "It's so good to see you."

"You too," Martha said, pulling back a bit to straighten her hair. "I know it's only been a few days, but it's weird not having you around."

"Are you at the deli?" Moira asked, recognizing the window sign behind her friend.

"We thought we'd stop in and see how things were going in your absence," Denise told her. "But it felt odd to be here without you, so we thought... why not bring you here too?"

"Hi, Ms. D," Meg said, popping into view behind the

deli owner's two friends. "How are you doing? Everything is great here."

"That's good to hear." She smiled at her employee, surprised at the pang of homesickness at the sight of all of the familiar faces. Even though she was having a good time on the cruise, she missed Maple Creek terribly. "I actually just won one of the challenges."

"Awesome!" Meg exclaimed. "We knew you'd do well, but it's still cool to hear. What did you make."

The deli owner grinned. "Lobster curry soup."

Denise chuckled. "I think that's something only you could pull off, Moira. So tell me, do you like the cruise? I might try to take a few weeks off sometime this winter, and it's been years since I've been on a cruise ship."

"I'm enjoying it," Moira told her friend. "The food is good, the rooms are clean, everyone seems really nice so far... I'm not sure what more I could ask for." *Other than no more mysterious deaths,* she thought, but she didn't say anything to her friends. Telling David was one thing, but Martha, Denise, and Meg would just worry.

"How's Candice?" Martha asked. "She doesn't have to do anything for the competition, right?"

"Right. I think she's enjoying herself. Who wouldn't be?" she chuckled. "She gets to go on a free ten-day cruise in the Caribbean."

"How are the people you're competing against?" her friend asked. "Are they nice?"

"Yeah, they have been pretty nice. The first guy to get disqualified seemed pretty upset, but that's understandable. I actually feel pretty bad for one of the other women. She got sick and couldn't stay in the competition anymore."

"Oh, how horrible."

"She was a really good cook, too," Moira said with a sigh. "She won the first round. You know what? I kind of want to go find her and see how she's doing. I had dinner with her last night, and I like her a lot."

"All right," Martha said. "It was good talking to you. You've got to tell us how you do tomorrow, okay? I bet you're going to win this thing."

"You've got this, Moira," Denise added. "If anyone deserves the prize, it's you."

# CHAPTER TWELVE

On her way out of her room to go look for Daphne, Moira ran into Candice.

"I was just coming to look for you," her daughter said. "I saw that today's challenge was over. How did it go?"

"Great." She grinned. "I won."

"No way! That's awesome. So that means no matter what, you can't be disqualified in the next round, right?"

"Right. Though the lady who won yesterday's challenge ended up dropping out today even though she had immunity. She's the one who got sick. I feel bad that she decided to drop out of the competition."

"She probably didn't want to risk working around food while she's sick," Candice said. "She could get the judges and you guys sick too."

"It seemed like she just had food poisoning," Moira said. "But I guess she knows best. I was about to go find her and see how she's doing. Do you want to come with me? It's Daphne, one of the people we had dinner with last night."

"Sure."

Together they wandered down the hall, not quite sure where to start their search. Since Daphne was in the competition, her room would be on the third floor, but there were no convenient name tags to help them figure out which one was hers.

"Does the ship have a hospital or anything?" Candice asked at last. "If she's really sick enough to drop out of the competition, maybe she's under the care of a doctor."

"The ship *does* have an infirmary," Moira remembered. "Xavier, the first mate, said as much when he was dealing with Bobby and his wife."

"Well, that should be easy to find, at least," the young woman replied. "Let's go find one of those maps."

A few minutes later they had oriented themselves around the 'you are here' sticker on the map in the hallway and were on their way to the infirmary on the main deck. It was easy to find once they knew where they were going, and Daphne welcomed them in to her small room.

"What happened?" Moira asked, looking at the pale woman in bed. "You were doing so well in the competition. We were all worried when you disappeared."

"I tried to work through," she told them. "But I kept feeling worse and worse, and I finally told Charlie that I needed to go. When I got here, the doctor wouldn't let me leave; he said he was concerned that I might have something contagious, and he didn't want to risk me spreading it to anyone else on the ship. I guess viruses spread quickly on cruises."

"I'm sorry, I know it must be terrible to have to drop out like you did," the deli owner said.

Daphne made a face. "You know; I feel bad enough that I don't even care about the competition. I just want to get better. And it would be great if my guts stopped trying to crawl out of my throat. Luckily one thing this boat has a lot of is anti-nausea medicine."

"You look a lot better than you did when you got up during dinner the other night," the Moira said. She was leaning against the wall, keeping a cautious distance away from the sick woman. The last thing she wanted was to catch Daphne's bug. "I hope whatever you had was just food poisoning and you'll be free to enjoy the rest of the cruise before you know it."

"Thanks," the other woman said. "I really think that's all I have myself, I guess the doctor is just being overly cautious. I told him it started right around dinner time, but he still thinks that the symptoms are too severe for regular food poisoning. I don't have much of a fever, though." She shrugged. "Either way, it was really nice of you to come visit me. You didn't have to; you should be out celebrating. I heard that you won today's challenge. Congratulations, by the way."

PATTI BENNING

"Thanks." The deli owner couldn't hold back her smile. "I hope you feel better, Daphne. It would be nice if all of us contestants could get together for one last dinner after the competition is over. I think all of us are good cooks, and we could really learn a lot from each other. We all share a passion for food, and would probably have a lot to talk about once we aren't so focused on winning this thing."

"Well, as long as I can keep the food down, I'd be happy to join you and whoever else for one last meal once this is all done," Daphne said. She smiled. "Now, go celebrate your win. Don't worry about me, I'll be fine."

Moira and Candice took her advice and went to go find a dining room serving an early dinner. The deli owner had once again skipped lunch, and she had been so anxious about the challenge that she hadn't eaten much for breakfast either.

They were debating whether to try one of the buffets

or a nice steak place overlooking the main deck when Nadine and her father, Doug, ran into them. The woman looked much better than she had at the end of the competition, and Moira was glad that she wasn't on the verge of tears anymore. The woman seemed nice enough, and it was obvious that the pressure of the competition had been getting to her.

"I'm glad we ran into each other," she told the two of them. "We were just looking for somewhere to eat. Do you want to join us?"

"Sure." Nadine gave her a hesitant smile. "Where were you thinking?"

"How about the steakhouse right over there?" she asked. "The food looks good, and they've got outdoor seating. Plus, it's early enough that they shouldn't be too crowded."

"Sure," the other woman said. "I'm hungry enough that I'd agree to pretty much anything."

"Hold on," Candice said. "I told Sofia I'd let her know where we're eating. I just have to send her a message really quick."

Twenty minutes later, Moira, Candice, Nadine, Doug, and Sofia were seated at one of the steakhouse's outdoor tables with a waiter taking their drink orders. A crisp breeze blew in from starboard, and they could hear strains of music from the deck above. It was a beautiful night.

"This is just like the first evening," Nadine said, taking a sip of her piña colada. "We're all sitting together again. It's nice."

"Except for Bobby and Linda," Moira said. "I still feel terrible about what happened to him, but things have just been so busy that I haven't really had time to process it."

"To the Babcocks," Sofia said, raising her drink. The rest of them toasted to that. Moira was about to add Daphne's name to another toast, but was interrupted by a familiar stranger.

"You guys have room for one more?" Antonio Cross asked gruffly. It hadn't been much more than a day since he lost the previous challenge, but he looked much the worse for wear to the deli owner. He hadn't shaved, and his eyes were bloodshot. She wasn't sure that she wanted him to join them, but it took her too long to think of a polite way to decline him. Sofia spoke up before she could.

"Sure, I'll scooch over, you pull up a chair," the young woman said, tugging her own chair over.

The man joined them, and an awkward silence

settled over the group. *Will it be weird if we talk about the competition and the next challenge with him here?* she wondered. *Just how upset is he about being the first one to be disqualified?*

The silence was broken at last by Candice, who cleared her throat and asked what everyone had spent the day doing. Moira relaxed as the small group began talking about poolside bars, the ship's theater, and the pod of dolphins Nadine and Doug had seen just after the competition. There was more to talk about than food, it seemed. Maybe the evening wouldn't be quite so awkward after all.

# CHAPTER THIRTEEN

The evening wore on slowly. The food was delicious, but somehow it didn't seem quite as good as the Redwood Grill back home. Moira missed her friend's restaurant and missed her own deli. She was glad that the cruise was only ten days long. How did some people stand going on two- or three-month cruises? She was enjoying the experience, but ached for something familiar. Even the stars looked different when they came out. The sky seemed endless, and the calm ocean below reflected it, eerily making it seem like they were floating in the heavens instead of on water.

"You know," Antonio said suddenly, surprising them all; he had been quiet for most of the meal. "I'm glad

I got disqualified. I don't have to deal with people judging everything I do for the next five days. I get to enjoy this." He gestured broadly to the sky and the sea. "I didn't need to win anyway. My restaurant is doing just fine. I only entered because my wife wanted a free cruise, then she ended up not coming anyway."

"I don't care about the cruise," said Sofia softly. Moira turned to look at her. The young woman had been quiet as well, even though Candice had tried a few times to draw her into the conversation. "This isn't a vacation for me. I need the money. My mom spent the last year battling cancer, and it's wiped out pretty much all of our savings. I need the ten grand to keep the restaurant and pay her hospital bills. We're in some pretty serious debt and... well, if I don't win this, I really don't know what we're going to do."

"I need the money too," Nadine said with a sigh as she put down her drink. "I said my husband was at home watching the kids... the truth is, he's leaving me. I've got to try to make it on my own as a single mom, while running a restaurant. Do you know how hard that's going to be?"

"I do, actually," the deli owner said with a glance at Candice. "I was a single mom too, though I didn't open the deli until Candice left for college. You'll get through it; just keep your chin up and don't be afraid to ask for help if you need it. I think you'll do just fine." She gave the other woman a reassuring smile that turned into a grimace as her stomach cramped.

"Are you okay, Mom?" Candice asked.

"I don't feel good," Moira told her. "Oh no, I hope I don't have what Daphne has. Maybe we shouldn't have visited her, after all."

"You should go to the doctor. Maybe you just ate something bad. Do you want me to come with you?"

She shook her head. "No, you stay here and enjoy the rest of the evening. I'm going to go lay down for a bit. Don't worry about me though, okay?" She forced a smile, which her daughter hesitantly returned.

"Okay, I guess," the young woman said.

"I hope you feel better," Nadine called after her as she left the table. "It would be terrible if you had to miss the next challenge."

"I'll do my best to be there," Moira managed to say through the cramps. "I'm sure a good night's rest is all I need to feel better."

Despite her brave words, her pain only got worse as she walked down to her room. *What is this?* she wondered. *Food poisoning? Or... could it be actual poisoning?* She frowned and tried to shake the thought away as pain-induced paranoia, but couldn't quite manage it. Now that she was thinking about it, it seemed like too great of a coincidence that both she and Daphne had gotten sick the evening after they won one of the challenges in the Chef War. Plus, there was poor Bobby, who had been killed before the competition had even started. Was it possible that someone was targeting the contestants?

"But who?" Moira muttered, shutting the door firmly behind herself before letting herself collapse into bed with a groan. Who would want to stop the competition? Who could possibly benefit from that? It wouldn't make sense if it was Damien or one of the judges—they had nothing to gain by wrecking the contest that they had created. It must be one of the competitors. Which meant that if this *was* poison, it must have been someone she was sitting with at dinner.

"What about Daphne, though?" she said, talking out loud in an effort to distract herself from the roiling in her belly. "Whoever poisoned me must have poisoned her, too. It's too much of a leap to guess that there are two people doing the poisoning. But none of the people I had dinner with tonight were there when I had dinner with her, except for Candice, and obviously she didn't do it."

If there was one person on the boat that she trusted, it was her daughter. *Maybe it isn't poison after all,* she thought as a particularly bad cramp ripped through her. *Maybe this really is just some terrible, terrible type of food poisoning.*

She dragged herself into the bathroom in hopes that a long, hot shower in the dark would help her feel better, or at least clear her brain for long enough for her to think. If she went to the doctor now, chances were she would be quarantined to the infirmary just like Daphne was, and she didn't want to risk that. *Don't be stupid,* she argued with herself as she turned on the water. *If you've really been poisoned, you need to see a doctor. There's no point in staying in the competition if you die.*

She reminded herself that Daphne seemed to be recovering well, and she hadn't been treated with anything except for anti-nausea medication. If this *was* poison it probably wasn't that strong a poison, or else the woman who had won the first challenge wouldn't be alive. *Unless she just got a smaller dose than I did.*

"Stop it," she muttered angrily to herself, hugging her knees to her chest as the hot water cascaded around her. "I need to *think* before I do something I might regret. If someone really is targeting the contestants and I go to the infirmary, dropping out of the competition, I'm just opening the door for another contestant to be hurt. On the other hand, if I'm wrong about all of this, and I just have a bad case of food poisoning, I would be throwing away the chance of winning ten thousand dollars and a spot on a cooking show with a celebrity chef because I have a few cramps. Either way, freaking out the ship's doctor is not going to help anyone."

Reluctantly, she decided to do her best to sit through the pain. The warm water seemed to be helping, and she let her mind wander back over her conversation with Daphne at dinner the other night. Had she said anything that might have indicated that someone had been acting weird around her? The deli owner didn't think so. The other woman had simply been happy after her win, and had been glad that everyone had been so nice during the competition. Everyone, that was, but Antonio Cross...

Moira gasped, opening her eyes wide in the dark shower. Daphne had said that she had run into Antonio last night before dinner, which meant that both of them had had contact with the man shortly before their stomach pain had started. Was it possible that Antonio was the one trying to hurt the contestants? And if so, did that mean that he had also murdered Bobby Babcock?

## CHAPTER FOURTEEN

"You're sure you're feeling better?" David asked.

"Yeah," Moira said, averting her gaze from the tablet's camera. "I'm fine this morning."

That was almost true. She had ordered enough painkillers and anti-nausea medication through room service to dull the cramps, but she still felt miserable after a fitful night's sleep. She was reluctant to tell David her true concerns about what she had described as food poisoning, but he seemed to have connected the lines himself.

"Are you sure you don't want to drop out of the competition?" he asked.

"Of course I don't. I want to win this thing. At the very least, I won't be scared away by some cheater."

He sighed and shook his head in exasperation. "I don't like this. Not when you're too far away for me to do anything to help you if things go south."

"I'll be careful," she promised him. "I always am."

"I'm not sure I believe that," he said, with the hint of a smile ghosting on his lips. "For someone who claims 'always to be careful,' you sure find yourself in a lot of trouble."

"Look, I'm on a ship with a lot of other people, and I promise not to go anywhere alone. I'll be fine. But

I've got to get going—it's time for the third challenge."

"Okay. I know that nothing I can say will stop you anyway. Good luck, Moira. You may not need it for cooking, but you definitely need it if someone's trying to get you out of the competition."

She closed the laptop and let the cheerful expression melt off her face. Her stomach *hurt.* She had no idea how she was going to get through the day. It was one thing to pretend to be fine while she was sitting at her desk; it would be another thing altogether to fake it while she was in the kitchen throwing together yet another haphazard recipe.

The five contestants met in the kitchen again. Moira scrutinized each of the others, wondering if anyone else was hiding symptoms of being poisoned. If they were, then they were better at faking it than she was; no one else seemed to be in pain, or to be suffering beyond the usual nervousness.

"Good morning, everyone," Charlie said in her usual cheerful tone when she strode through the kitchen's swinging doors. "I hope you're all excited and ready for the third challenge. I know the other guests have been enjoying watching the Chef War unfold each night, and I hope you have been having just as much fun competing with each other. I know it's early, but the sooner we get started, the sooner you'll find out who makes it to the next round... and who gets disqualified."

The five remaining contestants shared a wary look between themselves. The sure knowledge that one of them wouldn't be there tomorrow set them all on edge. Moira, thanks to her victory in the last round, was the only one safe from the possibility of being disqualified, but the pain she was suffering took away any relief that knowledge might have brought her.

"Today will be similar to yesterday's challenge in

that you will have a specific list of ingredients to use, but with a twist. You will each be responsible for choosing one ingredient, and you must do so without knowing what ingredients the others are choosing. This will give us a list of five randomly chosen ingredients that you each must use to create a unique dish. And you will only have half an hour to finish cooking it."

A few groans rose from the gathered group. Thirty minutes would be hard to achieve at the best of times. This challenge seemed like a disaster in the making to Moira. She resolved to choose the simplest ingredient that she could think of, and could only hope that the others would do the same.

"Please separate to your stations," Charlie said. "Each of you will find a pen and a piece of paper waiting for you. In a moment, I will ask you to write your chosen ingredient down, and I will come around and collect the papers. No talking, please. Nadine, you're responsible for choosing the meat. Hector, choose a spice. Moira, choose a fruit, Sofia

153

and Michelle, you both choose vegetables. Are you ready? Go."

The deli owner stared at the blank sheet of paper in front of her. She had to choose a fruit that they would all have to include in their dishes? She could hardly even think straight past the pain and nausea. Why hadn't she taken more of the pain pills before leaving her room?

*Come on, what fruit goes well with a lot of different things?* she thought. *Hmm... a tomato is technically a fruit, isn't it?* Wondering if she would be able to get away with it, she scribbled *tomato* on her piece of paper and folded it up. When Charlie came by, she handed it to her without a word.

"All right, you've all chosen," she said a moment later once she had made her circuit to each station. "This is the list of ingredients that must be included in your dishes. Trout, rosemary, tomatoes, okra, and zucchini. That doesn't sound too bad, does it? Now remember, points for creativity. And... begin."

Moira breathed a sigh of relief as the buzzer rang. The ingredient list really wasn't too bad. If she could actually think straight, she was sure she could come up with a unique and tasty dish utilizing those ingredients. As it was, since she couldn't be disqualified this round anyway, she decided to go the simple route and just make baked trout with a mixed vegetable side. While she was cooking, she would keep an eye on her fellow contestants and see if any of them were acting suspicious.

She got the trout in the oven first, then turned her attention to the vegetables, shooting surreptitious glances over at Sofia, who was to her immediate right. Last night, when the food poisoning or regular poisoning had been at its worst, she had been convinced that Antonio was the one responsible for all of this. He could easily have slipped something into her food or drink while they were eating, and he could have done the same to Daphne when they ran into each other the evening that the other woman

PATTI BENNING

had gotten sick. In the morning, however, when
things were clearer, she realized that it could have
been anyone. Just because Antonio was the most
obvious suspect didn't mean he was the only one
with a motive. Just last night, Sofia had told them
how desperate she was for the money. She didn't
want to believe that the friendly young woman who
seemed to get along so well with Candice could be
trying to get rid of the other competitors, but she
knew that ignoring a potential suspect would be
more than just foolish... it could be dangerous.


She spent so much time focusing on signs of suspicious activity from Sofia that she was shocked to
hear Charlie give the five-minute warning. She
opened the oven to take the trout out, and bit back a
curse. It had been left in too long, and while it wasn't
quite burnt to a crisp, she knew that there was no
way the overcooked piece of fish would win any
prizes that evening. Happy that she had her immunity to lean on, she did her best to make the plates of
food look nice, then followed the other contestants
out onto the ballroom floor.

# CHAPTER FIFTEEN

Considering how things had been going for her so far during the challenge, Moira shouldn't have been surprised to hear her name called first. She knew she couldn't be disqualified, but she still felt a hot rush of shame as the judges tore apart her dry, flavorless dish. She hadn't tried, and she knew it. She was too distracted by the fact that someone had tried to take three of the contestants out of the game, and had already succeeded with two of them. She was desperate to find out who was responsible before someone else got hurt, and she didn't know who she could go to on this ship. Who could she trust, other than Candice? There was no way she wanted to involve her daughter in this. As far as she knew, the ship didn't have any sort of police or law enforcement beyond a few security officers, and she didn't even know if she could trust them.

*What if all of this is for the contest?* she thought suddenly. *Before Daphne got sick, we were talking about how everyone was so much nicer than we were expecting. What if people were* too *nice? Competitions like this thrive on drama. Even though this is just a small time cooking competition that's only shown on this cruise ship, I bet Damien still makes a lot of money off of it. Passengers pay to be entertained while they're here, and people getting along and supporting each other doesn't make for good entertainment... but people getting poisoned and killed definitely does.*

She realized that everyone was staring at her. She must have been standing there silently for half a minute while she had her epiphany. *Maybe I took a few too many pain pills*, she thought.

"Sorry," she muttered, addressing the judges. "I'm

not feeling good. I think maybe I have what Daphne has."

She watched the three judges carefully, hoping for a sign, some flash of guilt, anything that would tell her that she was on the right track. Nothing.

"Maybe you should go back to your room and lie down," Damien suggested gently. "You do look rather pale. You won the last challenge, so you don't have to worry about being disqualified from this one."

"Okay... I think I will do that," she said. "Thank you, and sorry about the trout."

She walked out of the banquet hall, upset with herself for getting so distracted while she was cooking. She had every intention of doing something to continue her investigation, but when she reached her room she made the mistake of lying down on her bed. *Just a quick rest,* she told herself. Then she closed her eyes, and let exhaustion sweep her away.

When she woke up, the light coming through her room's one window was dim and gray. *I must have slept most of the day away,* she thought, horrified. *At least I feel better.* It was true. Whatever she had been suffering through for the last day seemed to have passed, and her mind was clear now that the pain and anti-nausea drugs had gotten out of her system. She still didn't know what was going on with her and Daphne's mysterious illness or Bobby's death, but she was determined to find out.

David answered the video call only seconds after she clicked the little green icon by his profile picture. She saw her own kitchen in the background, and smiled at the thought of him and the dogs there.

"You're not dead," he said.

"Did you think I was?"

"Well, you didn't answer my email, and you didn't call me to let me know how the third challenge went. I admit it was a passing concern, especially considering the fact that during our last conversation you were fighting off the effects of either food-poisoning or poison-poisoning that you refused to see the ship's doctor for."

"I... can see how you might have been worried." She heaved a sigh. "I'm sorry. Today was terrible. I ended up sleeping through most of it."

"Do you feel better?"

"Yes."

He smiled. "I'm glad. How did the challenge go?"

"I completely messed it up. I was too busy suspecting my fellow competitors of murder to even focus on cooking. My trout was overdone, and the veggie dish didn't even have any salt in it. I'm a failure."

"No, you aren't," he assured her. "You dragged yourself into the kitchen and gave it a shot instead of giving up. That's gumption."

"This whole trip is turning into a disaster," she groaned. "Why can't I ever just have a nice time without something bad happening?"

"Just take a deep breath, Moira," he said calmly. "Everything is going to be fine. I looked up your judges and the other contestants. None of them have priors. That doesn't mean none of them is the killer, but at least you know you aren't sharing the boat with hardened criminals."

"Or it means that whoever has been targeting the contestants is so good at what they do that they haven't ever gotten caught."

"I doubt that's the case. I think chances are you're dealing with someone who's just getting a bit too competitive. I take it you still aren't willing to drop out of the competition?"

"Not a chance," she said firmly.

He sighed, but didn't look surprised. "All right, let's take this one step at a time. Do you know who won the challenge today?"

"No. I literally just woke up. I don't even know where Candice is."

"Okay. Well, when you find out, keep your eye on them. From a distance, of course. If the person who won isn't the same person who poisoned you, chances are he or she will be the next target. Stay around groups of people, and for heaven's sake, don't go off on your own. I'll keep doing more research on the contestants in hopes that I can dig something up. Moira... be careful."

"I'll do my best," she told him.

She found Candice with Sofia in the closest buffet hall. She gave her daughter a quick hug, then sat down with them, declining the offer of food. She felt a lot better, but her stomach still wasn't a hundred percent and she didn't want to risk getting sick again.

"Sofia told me you weren't feeling well during the challenge, so I thought I'd let you sleep," Candice said. "I hope that's okay."

"That's fine, sweetie. I feel a lot better now. The extra

rest was probably good for me." She turned her attention to Sofia. "Did you win today's challenge?"

The young woman sighed. "No, I came in second place. That Hector guy won. Michelle got disqualified, and Nadine came in third. It's just the four of us tomorrow. Things are really starting to heat up."

"I bet," Moira muttered. "Do you know where Hector is?"

"No, why?"

"I think..." She hesitated, unsure whether or not she could trust the young woman in front of her. Out of the remaining contestants, Sofia seemed to have the most motive to try to cheat her way into winning. From the sound of it, she really needed the money to keep her business running, and that might be enough to drive her to murder.

"I just wanted to talk to him," she amended. "I might take a stroll around and see if I can find him. You two enjoy your dinner."

She gave the two young woman a tight smile and left. If Sofia was innocent, then Hector might be in grave danger. On the other hand, if the young woman was guilty, then she might just have left her daughter with a murderer.

# CHAPTER SIXTEEN

She was walking the main deck after twenty minutes of fruitless searching for Hector when she saw not him, but Antonio Cross. She paused, letting a strolling couple move ahead of her as she considered what to do next. All she had to go on right now was conjecture, and her list of suspects was a mile long. Should she take this opportunity and follow Antonio in case her original guess about him being the killer had been right, or would it be better for her to keep looking for Hector? What if Antonio led her to Hector?

She bit her lip, frozen in indecision. Just as Antonio was about to disappear around a bend, she leapt to follow him. Going with her gut had served her well in the first two cooking challenges; maybe it would serve her well now. There was no clearer suspect than the surly man who had been disqualified in the first round, and there was no way she could let him out of her sight until she knew for sure that he wasn't going to try to hurt anyone.

She followed as far behind him as she could, worried that if he knew she was there he might try to lose her... or worse, lead her into a secluded spot where he could ambush her. Luckily for her, it was still early enough that quite a few people were on deck admiring the stars and taking their time strolling down the walkway. It was easy to keep several people between them, and she doubted he would recognize her face in a crowd if he happened to look back.

Suddenly, unexpectedly, he sped up. Moira tried to follow him, but an older couple appeared out of nowhere in front of her and she had to stumble to a halt to avoid running into them. Muttering apologies, she inched her way past them, and let out a sharp sigh of annoyance. He was gone.

She hurried to the spot that he had disappeared and looked around, trying to guess a likely direction for him to have gone. Why did this cruise ship have to be so big and complicated?

She chose a direction at random and took a step toward an all-night bar when she heard a quickly cutoff shout coming from the other way. Her heart began racing. Had Antonio found Hector? Was she too late? She took off in the direction that she thought the shout had come from, and found herself in front of the closed door of a theater.

Hesitantly, she reached out and grasped the door handle. She wasn't certain that Antonio had gone in here—the shout could have come from further down the hall—but she couldn't pass the room without at least checking to see if the door was unlocked. Bracing herself, she pushed. It swung open silently at her touch.

She slipped inside the large room, letting the door close silently behind her, her eyes glued to the stage, which was only dimly lit by the night time lights. Two people stood on it. One was a hooded figure clothed in black—definitely not Antonio unless he had managed to change clothes in the space of a few seconds—and the other she recognized as Hector even from this distance. Hector was backing slowly toward the edge of the stage, his hands up.

*Now what?* wondered the deli owner desperately. She had found Hector in the nick of time, but had no way to save him. The theater was huge—there was no way she would be able to get down there in time, and even if she could, she had no weapons of her own. In the hand of the hooded figure she could clearly see the glint of some kind of blade. *Is this what happened to Bobby Babcock?* she found herself wondering, suddenly unable to get the gruesome image of the bleeding man out of her mind. She couldn't let that happen to someone else, she just couldn't.

An idea was beginning to form in her mind, but she

didn't know if she would have the time to implement it. She knew that the stage lights would be extremely bright, and if she could figure out how to turn them on she might be able to catch the killer unawares. She knew that her plan was partially flawed, since Hector would be just as blinded as the person threatening him with the knife, but it was her only option, short of charging the stage herself.

The only problem was, she had no idea where the switches for the stage lights were. There was likely some sort of control room, which was quite possibly locked. Even if she could find the right doorway, and it *wasn't* locked, what were the chances that she would hit the right switches on the first try?

She was out of time anyway. Hector had reached the edge of the stage, and could go no further without tumbling into the orchestral pit. It was a jump that he could easily make, but that would mean turning his back on the person who was slowly approaching him with the blade, which he was reluctant to do.

Desperate to prevent another death, Moira did the only thing she could think of.

"Hey, stop!" she shouted, her voice echoing in the huge, empty theater. Her ploy had the desired effect; the person with the knife lowered it a fraction of an inch and looked up, trying to find her among the dark seats. She had expected Hector to take this opportunity to leap down from the stage, but he appeared to be frozen in place.

"Go on, move," she muttered under her breath, but it was too late; the hooded figure was already turning back to him, evidently determined to finish what it had started before dealing with the new threat of Moira.

The hooded figure was only feet away from the terrified Hector when a third form rushed in suddenly from stage right. The person, whom she recognized as Antonio, slammed into the hooded figure, knocking him or her off the stage. The deli owner heard the sounds of a scuffle and then a shout, and saw the hooded figure take off toward one of the exits.

Concerned for both men, she hurried down to the stage to find Hector helping Antonio up. Her now-former prime suspect had a shallow cut on his upper arm, but otherwise seemed unharmed. The hooded figure had dropped his knife in panic as he fled.

"You saved my life," Hector was saying to Antonio in a shaky voice. "That psycho was going to kill me."

"It wasn't just me—Moira helped," Antonio said gruffly. "Without her shout, I might not have been able to get the drop on whoever that was."

"I didn't even know you were offstage," the deli owner admitted, shaken. "I... I thought that the hooded person was you."

"What?" Antonio looked at her, shocked. "Why?"

"Well, because whoever it is has been targeting people from the contest. You were the first to get disqualified, and you looked so upset, I thought..."

He snorted. "Well, you were wrong about that. But you were right about whoever it is targeting the contestants. I've been suspicious about the same thing since Daphne got sick, and you getting sick just solidified my suspicions. Hector was the logical next target, so I decided to follow him. I caught up with him in time to see him slip into this empty theater alone, and followed to see what was going on."

Moira frowned. "Why would you come in here?" she asked Hector.

"I heard someone ask for help," he told them. "It was a woman's voice. She called me by name, and I thought she sounded familiar, so I decided to check it out."

"Do you know who it was?" she asked.

"No... well, I do think it was one of the women from the contest, but I couldn't tell you which one if my life depended on it." He shuddered. "Sorry, bad choice of words."

Antonio looked up at her. "Well, it wasn't you, and it wasn't Daphne because she's still in the infirmary. That leaves Sofia, Nadine, and Michelle."

Moira paled. There were three possible murderers on the ship, and one of them was friends with her daughter.

# CHAPTER SEVENTEEN

The three of them agreed to split up. Hector would report what had happened to the security office. Antonio was going to go try to find the other women, and Moira was going to find her daughter. She was expecting a long search, and was surprised when she ran into Candice on her way back to their rooms.

"Mom, there you are. I was wondering where you went. Sofia decided to go to bed a little bit after you left, and I wanted to make sure you were okay before hitting the hay myself."

"Oh, my goodness, I was so worried about you," the deli owner said, enveloping her daughter in a hug.

"Why? What happened?" Candice asked, her forehead creasing with concern.

"Let's go back to our rooms, I'll tell you all about it there."

With their doors safely locked, Moira told her daughter all about her encounter with Hector, Antonio, and the mysterious hooded stranger.

"Someone is definitely trying to sabotage the competition," she said. "And at this point, I'm more concerned about keeping you safe than unmasking the bad guy. Will you promise me that you won't leave your room tonight?"

"Of course," Candice said. She raised an eyebrow. "Will you promise the same thing?"

The deli owner hesitated, but recognized the look in her daughter's eye. The young woman wasn't going to sit by while her mother roamed the halls with a killer running around, any more than Moira would be able to hide in her room with Candice out there. Keeping her daughter safe might mean staying holed up in her own room while someone else put their life on the line, but it was an easy choice to make. Her daughter would always come first.

"Yes," Moira said. "Neither of us will leave our rooms until morning, and then we go straight to the security office, together. Deal?"

"Deal."

"Good. Now, I'm going to go try to video call David and see if there's anything he can do from Michigan to help us here. You just sit tight, and get some sleep if you can."

She slipped through the door that joined their two rooms together and sat at her desk, bringing the tablet to life with the press of a button. Even though it was late, David answered her video call in a timely manner.

"Hey," he said, rubbing his eyes. "I'm surprised you're still up."

"I'm surprised *you're* still up," she replied.

"I've been doing research, like I promised," he told her. "I haven't found anything useful, though."

"That's okay," Moira said. "I have."

She told him about what had happened in the theater. When she was finished, they both fell silent for a moment, David shaking his head slowly.

"Don't leave your room," he warned her first.

"Of course I won't. I already made that promise to Candice. Is there anything you can do there? Would the police be able to help?"

He gave a grim laugh. "Moira, you are far, far out of the jurisdiction of any law enforcement agency I know. You're going to have to depend on whatever security they have on the ship to help you." He groaned. "I hate this."

"I know," she said. "Me too. I feel so helpless, I just—"

She broke off, something about his expression sending a jolt of fear through her.

"Moira," he said quietly. "Who's behind you?"

She spun around just as the woman lunged at her, nylon rope held tightly between her gloved hands. Moira avoided the loop of rope by pure chance, kicking out as the woman stumbled toward her. The force of their collision sent Moira into the desk, where the tablet fell over with a clatter, and the woman stumbled to one knee.

"Mom," Candice shouted from the next room. "Is everything okay?"

"Everything's fine, sweetie," Moira shouted back, determined to keep her daughter safe if it was the last thing she did.

The woman was beginning to get up. The deli owner tried to grab the rope from her, and a silent struggle ensued. In their throes, the woman's hood fell off, revealing not Sofia, but Nadine. The other woman yanked the rope out of Moira's hands as her grip went limp in surprise.

"You?" Moira blurted out, confused. "Why?"

"I need that money," Nadine hissed. "You'd do the same in my position."

Moira tensed, ready for the woman to reach for her with the rope again, but now that she had been identified and confronted, the other woman seemed less eager to attack her.

"No, I wouldn't," Moira whispered back, still determined to keep Candice from realizing that anything was wrong. "No amount of money is worth killing someone."

"Your kid is, though."

The deli owner blinked, confused. "I don't understand."

"My husband is leaving me, like I told you," Nadine said. To Moira's surprise, her voice cracked. "I need the money to hire a lawyer that will help me fight for my kids. Otherwise he's going to get full custody. I'd kill everyone on this ship if it meant I could keep my babies."

"Oh."

The deli owner let her hands drop, shocked by Nadine's revelation and shocked by her own reaction to it. It didn't excuse her murdering people, of course, but she couldn't help but feel some sort of bizarre sympathy toward the other woman.

"Don't look at me like that," Nadine grunted.

"Like what?"

"Like you care what happens. Like you could even begin to understand what I'm going through."

"Of course I can understand that, I'm a single mother, too," Moira said. "What was your plan, though? Just kill us all? Don't you think the judges would notice?"

"I didn't want to kill anyone," Nadine said, twisting the rope in her hands nervously. "Bobby... I lost control with him. At dinner that first night, he was bragging and bragging about how good his restaurant was and how many local contests he had won. I knew I couldn't beat him, and I panicked. But with you and Daphne, I was careful. I just gave you enough rat poison to make you sick."

"What about Hector?"

"He didn't eat with me," the other woman said plaintively. "I asked him to, and he refused. How else was

I going to slip poison to him? I know I'm not good at cooking, not like the rest of you. If you were all still around for the competition tomorrow, I would have been the next one disqualified. I had to act fast."

"I see," Moira said, striving for a soothing tone. "It's okay. Look, why don't you sit down? We can figure this out together. I—"

Without warning, the other woman lunged at her with the loop of rope, this time managing to slip it around Moira's neck and tighten it before she could get her fingers around it. The deli owner struggled, her panic making her stronger than usual, but even her fear couldn't overpower the other woman's determination. Her lungs aching, she began to see black spots in front of her eyes and she felt her arms losing strength as she scrabbled mindlessly at the rope around her neck. When the door between her room and Candice's room slammed open, the noise felt faint and distant, like a car door slamming far off.

A moment later, someone loosened the noose from around her neck and she thought she heard male voices talking, but she was too focused on the miraculous feeling of air coursing into her lungs to pay them any attention. Her throat ached, but she could breathe, and that was all that mattered.

## CHAPTER EIGHTEEN

"Thanks," she said hoarsely, reaching out to take the cup of warm tea and honey from the medic. Candice, who was sitting next to her on a bench in the infirmary, winced at the sound of her mother's voice.

"How bad does it hurt?" she asked.

"Worse than a cold. Not as bad as the fire," Moira said. The smoke inhalation from the barn fire a few weeks ago ranked as one of her worst experiences; even being choked into unconsciousness by a madwoman couldn't compare.

"That woman belongs in jail for the rest of her life," her daughter said, her hands still shaking with anger and fear. "She could have killed you."

"She *did* kill somebody," Moira pointed out. "I'm sure she'll get her jail time."

"She'd better," Candice muttered.

"What happened after she attacked me?" the deli owner asked. "I don't remember much. I blacked out toward the end."

"Well, when she came out of the bathroom behind you and you knocked the tablet over, David freaked out and video called me. He told me to phone security, which I did, then he had me listen at the door. At first it didn't seem like you needed help, but then she started choking you so I rushed in and started trying to pry her hands off the rope. Then security got there and took over, and the medics rushed you to the infirmary and got you to wake up and... here you are."

"I don't know whether to be glad that you saved me, or mad that you put yourself in danger," Moira said with a sheepish grin. "I think I'm a little bit of both. You aren't ever supposed to put yourself in danger for me. But, you know, thanks for not letting me die."

"Mom, you can't really think I was going to let some crazy lady kill you."

"I know." She grinned at her daughter. "You're too much like me for that to happen."

The second annual Grand Cruise Chef War was immediately cancelled the moment that Damien Warner heard about Nadine's attacks. Moira wasn't surprised, but was a bit disappointed that after everything she had been through, she wouldn't have a chance to finish pitting her skills against those of the other cooks. She was surprised when Damien called all the contestants to the banquet hall, two days after her attack. Nadine was handcuffed in the security office and would remain there until they docked at a port.

"I want to extend my deepest condolences to all of you," Damien told them once they had gathered. "None of this should have happened, and I cannot apologize enough for failing to keep you safe. Those of you that want to go home early, I will personally pay for your airfare. Those of you who want to stay, please do so, but the contest is officially over. That said, there is still the matter of the prize money."

A few heads went up at that.

"As we were unable to complete the challenges, it's impossible to name a winner. And since some of you were incapacitated during a couple of the challenges, I feel it's only fair to disregard those results.

But as far as I'm concerned, each and every one of you is a stellar chef, and so I've decided to split the prize money six ways. You'll each be getting a share, and Linda Babcock will be receiving her husband's portion."

There were a few happy murmurs amongst the group. Split six ways, ten thousand dollars would be just over sixteen hundred dollars each. It wasn't a ton of money, but it was better than leaving with nothing, and none of them wanted to have anything to do with the competition for longer than necessary, now that they knew for sure about the murder and the poisonings.

Moira opted to go home early. She just couldn't see enjoying the rest of the cruise after everything that had happened, and Candice agreed that the best place to recover would be back in Maple Creek with their loved ones. By the time the ship neared a Haitian port, they had their bags packed and were ready to disembark for good. Before making her way off the boat, the deli owner had one last thing she wanted to do; she found Sofia and handed her the envelope with her portion of the winnings in it.

"I know it isn't much, but you deserve it," Moira told her. "Use the money to help keep your business running."

"Oh, no, I couldn't—"

"Please," the deli owner said. "I don't need it, but you do. I know it's not easy to run a small business, so let me do what I can to help."

"If... if you're sure," Sofia said hesitantly.

"Take it." Moira smiled. "And if you're ever in Michigan, stop by my deli and say hi."

"Or my candy shop," Candice added. "You're

welcome to visit any time."

"Thank you two so much," the young woman said, throwing her arms around them both. "I never thought I'd make such good friends on this trip. I promise to stay in touch."

"So do I," Candice said. "Maybe I can take a road trip out west to visit you next summer."

"Yes," Sofia squealed. "That would be amazing. And once I get things settled, I can return the favor. I'm so glad I went on this cruise, despite everything. It's nice to know that there are people out there like you. I really feel like things are going to work out now."

They waved at her as they left the cruise, each feeling ambivalent about the events of their aborted vacation. Parts of it had been wonderful, and parts had been horrifying. Moira knew that they would both be glad to get home.

ALSO BY PATTI BENNING

**Papa Pacelli's Series**

Book 1: Pall Bearers and Pepperoni

Book 2: Bacon Cheddar Murder

Book 3: Very Veggie Murder

Book 4: Italian Wedding Murder

Book 5: Smoked Gouda Murder

Book 6: Gourmet Holiday Murder

Book 7: Four Cheese Murder

Book 8: Hand Tossed Murder

Book 9: Exotic Pizza Murder

Book 10: Fiesta Pizza Murder

Book 11: Garlic Artichoke Murder

Book 12: On the Wings of Murder

Book 13: Mozzarella and Murder

Book 14: A Thin Crust of Murder

Book 33: Murder, My Darling

**Killer Cookie Series**

Book 1: Killer Caramel Cookies

Book 2: Killer Halloween Cookies

Book 3: Killer Maple Cookies

Book 4: Crunchy Christmas Murder

Book 5: Killer Valentine Cookies

**Asheville Meadows Series**

Book 1: Small Town Murder

Book 2: Murder on Aisle Three

Book 3: The Heart of Murder

Book 4: Dating is Murder

Book 5: Dying to Cook

Book 6: Food, Family and Murder

Book 7: Fish, Chips and Murder

**Cozy Mystery Tails of Alaska**

Book 1: Mushing is Murder

# AUTHOR'S NOTE

I'd love to hear your thoughts on my books, the storylines, and anything else that you'd like to comment on—reader feedback is very important to me. My contact information, along with some other helpful links, is listed on the next page. If you'd like to be on my list of "folks to contact" with updates, release and sales notifications, etc.... just shoot me an email and let me know. Thanks for reading!

Also...

... if you're looking for more great reads, Summer Prescott Books publishes several popular series by outstanding Cozy Mystery authors.

# CONTACT SUMMER PRESCOTT
## BOOKS PUBLISHING

Twitter: @summerprescott1

Bookbub:
https://www.bookbub.com/authors/summer-prescott

Blog and Book Catalog:
http://summerprescottbooks.com

Email: summer.prescott.cozies@gmail.com

YouTube:
https://www.youtube.com/channel/UCngKNUkDd
WuQ5k7-Vkfrp6A

And...be sure to check out the Summer Prescott Cozy Mysteries fan page and Summer Prescott Books Publishing Page on Facebook – let's be friends!

To download a free book, and sign up for our fun and exciting newsletter, which will give you opportunities to win prizes and swag, enter contests, and be the first to know about New Releases, click here: http://summerprescottbooks.com

Made in the USA
Las Vegas, NV
30 January 2025

17227011R00115